Tears of a Hustler 5

The Spades

A Novel

Silk White

GOOD2GO PUBLISHING

Good2go Publishing

This novel is a work of fiction. All the characters, organizations, establishments, and events portrayed in this novel are either product of the author's imagination or are fiction.

GOOD2GO PUBLISHING
7311 W. Glass Lane
Laveen, AZ 85339

www.good2gopublishing.com
twitter @good2gobooks
G2G@good2gopublishing.com
Facebook.com/good2gopublishing
ThirdLane Marketing: Brian James
Brian@good2gopublishing.com
Cover design: Davida Baldwin
Typesetter: Rukyyah
ISBN:
Printed in the United States of America

Acknowledgements

To you reading this right now. Thank you for stepping inside the bookstore, stopping by the library, or downloading a copy of Tears of a hustler 5. I hope you enjoyed this read from top to bottom. My goal is to get better and better with each story. I want to thank everyone for all their love and support. It is definitely appreciated! Now without further ado ladies and gentleman, I give you **"TEARS OF A HUSTLER 5"**. ENJOY!!!

Silk White

INTRO

Pauleena stood in the chow line in the mess hall on point and alert. This jail shit wasn't something that Pauleena could see herself getting used to. Surrounded by a bunch of racist female C.O.s was one thing, but the bum bitches that stood around telling lies all day was what irritated Pauleena the most. To go from living a luxury type of life to living like a peasant didn't sit well with her. Her expensive designer name clothes were replaced with a tan Dickie suit and a pair of black boots that hurt her feet and turned her socks black.

Pauleena glanced around the mess hall and felt like all eyes were on her. She knew her face had been in the papers and all over the news so it was no secret that everyone in the entire jail knew who she was, what she was about, and how she got down. Even the police seemed to be keeping a close eye on her.

Pauleena could care less who watched her, she was there to do her time and go home. Being told what to do, when to do it, and how to do it was one of the things that she would have to adjust to for the time being.

A fat brown skin chick handed Pauleena her tray. Pauleena's eyes immediately glanced down at the tray. Two hot dogs, cold stale looking tater tots, peas, and Jello decorated the tray.

Pauleena sat down at the next available seat at the table and noticed all of the other inmates gobbling down their food. The way they were eating one would have thought a five star chef had prepared the meal and not a civilian cook who made the inmates do all the cooking. Pauleena shook her head and nibbled on one of the cold tater tots. As she chewed down on her food she noticed two chicks who were sitting across from her staring a hole through her. At first Pauleena took the two chicks as groupies who were happy and excited to say that they had finally met somebody that they had seen all over the TV, but the two chicks weren't groupies at all. Instead they were members of The Spades organization.

The two women had been personally handpicked to join The Spades organization by Wolf himself. When the police went on their spree of locking up any and everybody who had anything to do with The Spades, the two women who were named Tina and Jessica got picked up during the sweeps. They knew just who Pauleena was and what she stood for and quite frankly it disgusted them.

Once Tina and Jessica heard that Pauleena had been transferred to the same jail that they were in, they knew that shit was sure to get ugly sooner than later. This was Tina and Jessica's first time seeing Pauleena up close and personal and they weren't impressed to say the least. In their eyes she was just a regular chick trying to be something that she wasn't. Throughout the entire jail there were close to a hundred and fifty female Spades members, so if Pauleena thought she was just going to do a smooth four years she had another thing coming.

Pauleena bit down into her hot dog, looked up and noticed the two chicks who sat across from her staring at her with mean looks on their faces.

"What?" Pauleena asked.

"What; what?" The woman that went by the name Tina countered aggressively.

"I mean, I see you and your home girl staring at me and all that. I wanted to see what was up," Pauleena said. "Ya'll know me from somewhere or something?"

"Yeah we looking at you and..." Tina's entire body language was hostile; changing the vibe of the conversation. "You talking like you wanna do something about it."

Realizing that she was outnumbered, Pauleena bowed out. "Listen," she began. "I don't want no trouble."

"You should have thought about that before you decided to go up against The Spades," Tina growled. The only thing that stopped her from punching Pauleena dead in her mouth right then and there was a passing C.O.

Pauleena flashed a smile. "You two are Spades?"

"You already know and just so you know, Wolf ain't too happy about you still supplying the streets with work," Tina told her.

Pauleena continued to smile. "I'm sorry to hear that." She could give two fucks about Wolf and how he felt. She would deal with Wolf personally once she was released from jail. The beef between her and The Spades would go on forever until either she or Wolf was killed.

Over Pauleena's shoulder, Tina spotted two other members of The Spades. Seeing them helped to build her confidence and change the whole way she was coming at Pauleena.

"Something funny," Tina said. Before Pauleena could fix her mouth to respond, Tina reached across the table and smacked the shit out of Pauleena causing her face to forcefully snap to the right. After Tina slapped Pauleena, Jessica reached over the table and snatched all of the tater tots from off of Pauleena's tray.

"Ain't nobody playing with you in here bitch," Tina growled. She was all the way turned up and ready to go wherever Pauleena wanted to take it.

Pauleena touched the corner of her mouth with her tongue and tasted blood. The slap really caught her off guard. Pauleena and Tina exchanged stares.

"You got a problem then pop off," Tina said ready to go.

"You got it," Pauleena said humbly.

"Yeah I know I got it bitch," Tina said confidently. She was twice Pauleena's size and had already played out in her head a dozen times what she would do to Pauleena if she even thought about acting like she was tough.

Pauleena stood up and acted like she was about to leave, but then quickly spun and slapped Tina across the face with her tray. This move caused the entire mess hall to erupt in a loud roar. Once things started to pop off Jessica hopped across the table and charged Pauleena with her arms swinging. Jessica and Pauleena exchanged punches before a third party jumped in the fight, attacking Pauleena from behind. The third woman tried to put Pauleena in a choke hold, but Pauleena wasn't going out without a fight. She scratched and clawed the third woman's eyes, while Jessica landed several hard blows to Pauleena's stomach. Pauleena grabbed a handful of her hair and threw several hard blows.

Pauleena used all of her energy and slammed the third woman up on the table causing a loud bang.

Now the rest of the female inmates stood yelling and cheering like they were at a Mayweather fight. The fight had turned the entire mess hall into a frenzy. When Tina finally regrouped, she quickly jumped in the fight and joined the action. It quickly turned from a two on one, to a three on one. The three women finally wrestled Pauleena down to the floor and began kicking and stomping her out.

"The Spades run shit around here bitch!" Tina huffed as she brought the heel of her boot down on Pauleena's face. She was stomping her face down onto the cold and dirty mess hall floor.

Pauleena laid out on the floor in a fetal position; balled up covering her body as best she could. The trio continued to kick and stomp Pauleena out until several C.O.'s came and separated the trio from a wounded Pauleena. She was down and her long hair was loose from being pulled during the fight. Her tan Dickie shirt was missing several buttons.

The C.O.'s made each and every inmate lie down on the floor, face first while they regained control of the situation. Each woman that was involved in the brawl was then hand cuffed and roughly escorted to the S.H.U. (Special Housing Unit) better known as the box.

"You better get used to seeing my face," Tina yelled while being escorted out of the mess hall.

If Tina and the rest of them Spades bitches thought that they could put hands and feet on Pauleena and get away with it, then they were in for a rude awakening. Pauleena wasn't the one to fuck with. The Spades as well as the rest of the jail were about to find out the hard way.

TEARS OF A HUSTLER 5

THE SPADES

Chapter One

CALLER ID

"Yes hello. My boyfriend over here acting a damn fool," a woman named Pat said into her cell phone. "He's drunk talking about he's not leaving," she continued. "I want him out of my house. Can you please send some Spades over here to get him to leave cause I got two little kids over here and I don't want no trouble."

"Yes ma'am we have a van in that area. Stay calm and The Spades will be there in no time," the operator for The Spades said in a friendly tone.

"Well hurry up cause I don't want him to try and take this pussy," Pat said into the phone before ending the call.

Once Pat hung up she turned and faced Prince with her hand out. "Okay. I did what you asked. Now where's my bread?"

Prince nodded towards Tall Man and he immediately placed five hundred dollars in her hand.

"Get up outta here Pat," Prince told her. He didn't want her around when The Spades showed up. The Spades called themselves patrolling and policing their community. Instead of dialing 911 The Spades had some how convinced and brain washed the community to call The Spades instead of the police when an emergency presented itself. They had a nice little system working for them. Too bad for them that Prince and Psycho were on a mission to kill as many Spades as possible until there were no more Spades left to kill. Pauleena may have been locked up, but that wasn't going to stop the movement from moving. Before she left, she put Psycho and Prince in charge of running things until she returned. While Pauleena was away she knew that her empire was left in good hands. She also knew that with Prince and Psycho running things that they would make a ton of money as well as kill as many Spades as they possibly could. Either way it was a win, win.

Prince and Tall Man sat around politicking when a sharp knock at the door interrupted the two's conversation. Prince removed his .40 cal from his waist and held it with a two-handed grip as he inched his way towards the door. Prince gave Tall Man a silent nod. Tall man quickly snatched open the door using it as a shield. Once the door swung open, Prince put a bullet in the two Spades member's head that stood on the other side of the door. The two Spades members fell down to the floor before they even had a chance to figure out what was going on.

"We out," Prince said as him and Tall Man stepped over the two dead bodies and made their exit. There was no way no man was going to tell Prince he couldn't get any money. He didn't care if it were a million Spades members out there. If they didn't want him getting money then they were going to have to kill him ,point blank period.

Prince was tired of The Spades running around like they were invincible. The only advantage The Spades had over Prince and his team was that there were just as many Spades running around willing to die for whatever Wolf said. Prince silently wondered where Wolf found all these loyal people who were willing to die over a cause that he made up.

None of the mattered cause Prince planned on clapping anybody affiliated with The Spades, no questions asked. It was to the point where too much had happened to end the war that was going on right now. If innocent blood had to be shed to get a point across then so be it.

Prince touched the scar on his face as he sat in the passenger seat. Not only were Prince and Psycho going up against The Spades, but they also had The Real Spades to worry about. Live Wire was still at the top of Prince's hit list. Every day that he looked in the mirror and saw the scar on his face, it reminded him of the beef between him and Live Wire.

"What you over there thinking about?" Tall Man asked glancing over at Prince. Him and Prince had been rolling tough for a while now so he pretty much knew when something was wrong with Prince.

"I want to kill this clown ass nigga Live Wire so bad," Prince said with plenty of emotion. If it was one thing that Prince hated, it was a nigga who was soft, but acted tough, acted as if he was with whatever, but really not. In his eyes that was Live Wire. He was all mouth with no action. "I mean I don't even know how a clown like him even lasted this long." He shook his head.

"Don't worry about it," Tall Man said in a calm voice and smooth tone. "We gon bump into that clown soon," he told him. "He can't hide forever, but until we run into that Bozo we continue to take out as many Spades as we can."

Prince nodded his head. His phone buzzing notified him that he had received a text message. He glanced down at the screen and saw that he had a message from Psycho.

Psycho: *Talk to me and I'll talk back.*

Prince: *Seven down so far, but the night is still young.*

Psycho: *Still no sign of Wolf?*

Prince: *Nope*

Psycho: *What about Live Wire or the new nigga in charge of the Spades Dice?*

Prince: *These sorry ass niggaz ain't nowhere to be found.....SMH but what you getting into for the night?"*

Psycho: *At the warehouse with this crazy nigga Bobby Dread....LOL swing through*

Prince: *OMW (on my way)*

With that being said Tall Man made a detour and headed towards the warehouse. Prince could only imagine what Psycho and Bobby Dread had up their sleeves for the night. Prince noticed that Pauleena's absence had really been affecting Psycho lately. He couldn't put his finger on it, but Psycho hadn't been the same ever since Pauleena had been removed from the streets and put in jail.

Prince could only imagine what it was like to have his significant other locked away in a cage like an animal, so he could only imagine what Psycho was going through right now.

Tall Man pulled the Charger up into the entry of the warehouse and then killed the engine along with the lights. He didn't know what Prince's plans for the night were, but he was done for the night. A nice thick chocolate thing awaited his return back at his apartment. Within the next hour he planned on being under the sheets in between some warm thighs.

Prince and Tall Man entered the warehouse and immediately covered their noses. Inside the warehouse Bobby Dread walked around shirtless with a bloody baseball bat in his hands. Several rough looking Jamaicans stood around along with Psycho watching Bobby Dread do what he did best.

In front of Bobby Dread sat three Spades members. They sat naked, tied down to a fold out chair; three Spades members in three different chairs. Psycho was sick and tired of trying to figure out where the Spades new headquarters was located. The Spades were still out on the streets knocking off as many drug dealers as they could. The war against good and evil was nowhere near ending. The longer the war went on, the more it pissed Psycho off.

"Where's that punk motherfucker Dice hiding at?" Bobby Dread asked The Spades member who sat in chair number one. Unlike everyone else Bobby Dread was enjoying the ongoing war between the Hustler's and The Spades. Putting in work and hurting people was his thing and what he did best.

"Fuck you!" chair number one said. He used all his strength and might and tried to break free of the rope that kept him connected to the chair, but it was no use. The only place he would be going was to an early grave.

Bobby Dread gripped the baseball bat tight and then swung with all his might. The bat sounded like it made flush contact with a hundred miles an hour fast ball. Bobby Dread didn't stop there, he continued beating The Spades lifeless body with the baseball bat until he ran out of energy.

Bobby Dread let the bat hang down by his side and walked over to The Spades member that sat in chair number two. "Where's The Spades new headquarters located?"

"Go fuck yourself!" was The Spades members response. His eyes showed no fear, telling the man who stood before him that he was prepared to die if necessary.

Prince turned his head as Bobby Dread's bat made contact with chair number two's head. "How's Pauleena been holding up on the inside?" he asked Psycho as the sound of the bat repeatedly making contact with a skull sounded off throughout the warehouse.

"She's hanging in there," Psycho replied. His cell phone buzzing down on his hip grabbed his attention for a split second. He glanced down at the screen on his phone and quickly hit the ignore button. "I'm going up there to see her next week."

"When you see her tell her I send my love," Prince said. Deep down inside he too missed Pauleena. Shit just wasn't the same with her gone. Prince knew if Pauleena was home right now, a lot of shit would be different. "She need some bread or anything?"

"Nah, her books are filled up," Psycho answered. While his woman was in jail she wouldn't want or need for anything, especially while he was still breathing and had his freedom. "I think she might be in the box."

"Why you say that?"

Again Psycho's phone buzzed and again he hit the ignore button and continued where he left off. "She hasn't called me in a few days and that's unlike her."

"That's crazy," was all Prince said. He was no stranger when it came to jail so he knew how one minute things could be cool and then the next you were sitting in the box looking stupid. "You think something popped off in there?"

Psycho shrugged. "I don't know," he said honestly. "I know The Spades are deep in the prison system," he pointed out. "If something did pop off, I know my baby can handle herself."

The sound of Bobby Dread's bat making contact with The Spades member that sat in chair number three's head caused both Prince and Psycho to wince as if it were them getting hit with the wooden baseball bat. Psycho knew that Bobby Dread wouldn't stop until each and every last member of The Spades were dead.

"What you got planned for the rest of the night?" Psycho asked while his cell phone buzzed again down on his hip causing Prince's eyes to go from looking at him down to the cell phone that rested on his hip.

"You gon answer that?" Prince asked with a suspiciously raised eye brow. He didn't know who was trying to get in touch with Psycho, but whoever it was; they were blowing his phone up.

Psycho hit the ignore button on his phone again. "Nah, it ain't nobody but that clown Mr. Goldberg. I deaded him on some bread that I still owe him from Pauleena's case," he lied. The truth was he didn't want Prince all in his business. Whoever was calling him was none of Prince's concern.

"Them fucking lawyers are worse than stick up kids." Prince said, "Be careful, them Jews be mad grimy."

"I ain't worried about that clown," Psycho said brushing the situation off. "But yo, I'mma holla at you tomorrow," he said giving Prince a pound. "If you run into one of them Spades hit me up and keep an eye on Bobby Dread for me." Psycho said, and then exited the warehouse.

Chapter Two

Caught Up

Psycho cruised down the highway in his all black Audi while the sound of Jim Jones new mix tape bumped in the car's speakers at an even volume. He had a lot on his mind and even more on his plate especially with Pauleena being locked up. It was him who was responsible for taking care of and handling everything from the finances, the product, and even the distribution. On top of all of the outside distractions Psycho missed Pauleena a lot, more than he cared to admit, but the truth was his woman being away was killing him.

Psycho kept his eyes on the road, but the buzzing of his cell phone caused him to pick up his phone and answer it. "What!?" He barked into the phone. "I'll be there in five minutes," Psycho said ending the call, not even giving the caller on the other line a chance to reply. The caller was really beginning to piss Psycho off to the point where he was ready to cut out all ties with the caller.

Psycho already had a lot going on and he didn't need any more stress added on to his already stressful life. Things were already bad enough, so to complicate things even further wouldn't be a wise move.

Psycho parallel parked in front of a project building out in Queens, grabbed his .45 from off the passenger seat, tucked it down into his waistband and hopped out. Psycho knew moving around alone wasn't a wise move being as though The Spades, The Real Spades, stick up kids, as well as the police were out to put a bullet in his head, but at the moment he wasn't worried or concerned about any of that. If anybody ran up on him he planned on holding court in the streets.

The closer Psycho made it to the building, he could see several men standing around in the lobby loitering and looking out for potential fiends looking to buy their drug of choice.

Psycho reached the lobby and immediately one of the rough looking men who wore a red bandana tied around his head buzzed him into the building.

"Bang, bang. What up?" Psycho asked giving the fake brolick man a pound. "How it's looking out here?"

"Slow motion," Bang replied. His eyes immediately landed on the expensive looking chain that hung around Psycho's neck.

"You keeping these niggaz in line out here?"

"You already know," responded Bang. He was known for letting his hammer off and well respected throughout the five boroughs. "Niggaz told me they saw Live Wire and a few of them Real Spades niggaz around here the other day," Bang said. "Said them niggaz was gripped up something crazy too."

"Them niggaz better be strapped when I run into them." Psycho gave Bang dap and then disappeared on the elevator. He didn't have time to sit around and talk to Bang all night, at the moment he had something more important to take care of that needed his immediate attention.

When Psycho stepped off the elevator the first thing he heard was loud music. The walls were damn near vibrating from the bass coming out of the apartment he was headed for. A track from Gucci Mane's mix tape "Trap God" could be heard as clear as day.

Psycho reached the door with the loud music and knocked on the door hard like he was the police. After three minutes of knocking the volume of the music could be heard coming down to a more reasonable level. Seconds later the sound of the locks being unlocked could be heard followed by the door easing open.

On the other side of the door stood a brown skin sexy thing who favored the actress Nia Long. The Nia Long look alike stood bare foot wearing nothing, but a white wife beater that while pulled down barely covered the top part of her nice sized ass and round hips. She had an angry looking scrawl on her face. Her heavily glossed lips shined brightly adding to her sex appeal.

"What the fuck you out in the streets doing that's so important that you can't answer your motherfucking phone?" She said with venom dripping from her tone. "You ain't see me calling you? Huh? Now niggaz is blind," she went on. "That's that bullshit I be talking about."

Psycho entered the apartment and slammed the door behind him. "What the fuck I told you about calling me back to back Monica?" He growled getting all up in Monica's face. He so badly wanted to smack the shit out of her. "I told you if I don't answer then that means I'm busy and I'll hit you back as soon as I can."

"So, you been busy all motherfucking day, that's what you telling me?" Monica huffed. "So busy that you can't pick up the phone for one second and just say baby I'm a little busy right now and I'll hit you back? Miss me with that dumb shit. Not even Obama is *that* busy."

"Listen," Psycho sighed loudly pinching the bridge if his nose. "If you want to continue to see me, then you gon have to tone down that nasty ass attitude of yours," he told her. "We already playing a risky game," he reminded her.

Monica looked at Psycho as if he had called her a name. "Nigga you can't be serious," she raved. "Ain't nobody scared of your *little* girlfriend Pauleena, but you! Okay, so she sells a *little* drugs big deal," Monica went on. "I tell you what though, if that bitch ever barks up my tree she getting knocked the fuck out, but I bet if that bitch called you, I bet you'd do a back flip and jump through a ring of fire to answer your phone then. FUCK OUTTA HERE!"

Psycho ignored all of Monica's tough talking and threats. It was obvious that she didn't know much about Pauleena, because if she did she damn sure wouldn't be talking so reckless. Psycho had tried to leave Monica several times, but Monica's freakiness is the only thing that kept him around for so long. He knew fooling around with her was wrong, but the things she did to him sexually made it all right.

"Watch ya mouth."

"Or else what?" Monica challenged.

"I can't," Psycho said simply. He spun away from Monica and headed for the door. He didn't have time to deal with her ratchetness. The worst part was Psycho knew better than to deal with a woman like Monica in the first place, especially having a good woman like Pauleena by his side. Yeah Pauleena may have been a little violent and rough around the edges, but she was loyal and probably as loyal as they came. That's why Psycho did his best to keep him and Monica's relationship a secret. He couldn't afford for his business to be put in the streets in fear of word getting back to Pauleena. Psycho knew how people loved to gossip and add on to the story. If the story of his relationship with Monica ever got out there Psycho knew by the time Pauleena heard the story it would be ten times worse than the reality of it. Along with ten times more lies added on to the already bad story, so Psycho's main objective was to keep him and Monica's business between him and Monica.

Monica dashed around Psycho in a flash and stood in front of the door denying him access to leave her apartment.

"I don't got time for this shit! Me and you are done! Now move," Psycho said seriously. He was sick and tired of Monica and her ignorant ways. Not to mention he really did love Pauleena and deep down inside he felt bad about cheating on her especially while she was locked up. She was depending on him to be faithful to her and that was the least he could do. *"You playing yourself,"* he silently thought to himself while looking down at Monica.

"I'm sorry baby. Please don't leave me," Monica said in a toddler like voice. "I don't know what's wrong with me. I just get so crazy when it comes to you. When you don't answer your phone, my mind automatically assumes that you are out with another woman. You know every man I've had my whole life has cheated on me," Monica said pushing out some tears. At that very moment she deserved an academy award for her performance. "I'm sorry baby. Please don't leave me," she begged.

"Move from out front of the door," Psycho said dryly. "I don't got time for you and your fake ass tears."

"Fake ass tears?" Monica echoed. "Can't you see that I love you? Can't you see that I only act like this because I love you?" She grabbed Psycho and pulled him in close for a hug and the scent from his Bleu de Chanel cologne flirted with her nostrils.

"Can you give me one more chance........pleeeeeeeeeeeeeease?" Monica purred. She stood on her tippy toes and gently kissed Psycho's lips. "Please don't leave me. I promise I'll be a good girl," her lips said softly as her eyes begged him.

Before Psycho got a chance to reply, Monica had already melted down to her knees and was already pulling out his dick. She circled her thumb around the tip of Psycho's dick and played with his pre-cum while gently fondling his balls with her free hand. Monica looked up into Psycho's eyes from down on her knees. "If you cum in my mouth, I promise I'll be good and I promise to swallow all of it like a big girl."

Psycho was in love with the way that Monica handled her business behind closed doors. The nasty things that came out of her mouth were what turned Psycho on the most. Not to mention when it came to oral sex Monica was at the top of her class; maybe even in a class of her own.

Monica wrapped her shiny, heavily glossed lips slowly around the head of Psycho's dick and inhaled gently. Gradually she opened her mouth wider and slid it farther and farther into her mouth until his dick had completely disappeared and she could feel his balls touching her chin. She slowly dragged his full length out of her mouth while slurping on it like it was a Popsicle on a sunny day.

"Oooh shit," Psycho whispered with his eyes closed. He ran his fingers through Monica's hair and enjoyed her mouth. Monica made wet nasty sounds, her head rising and falling in a slow deliberate rhythm. She was massaging and sucking, sucking and stroking, performing like a wild porn star. Monica licked, sucked, and slurped on Psycho's dick like a woman possessed until an eruption exploded inside her mouth.

Monica gave Psycho's dick one last long slurp before she swallowed and let out a light moan as if her thirst had finally been quenched. After her performance Monica knew she had Psycho right where she wanted him. She slowly crawled back up to her feet looking at Psycho with pleading eyes. Monica turned, lifted her wife beater up slightly and hiked her ass up in the air. "Come get in this pussy."

Psycho took Monica right there on the floor. He turned Monica on her stomach, kept her legs closed, straddled her, and crawled inside of her hot and wet slice. Monica frowned back at what was going in and out of her and stared at it with moans and a few grunts. Her skin slapping against his sounded like the ultimate battle. Psycho may have been there physically, but mentally his mind was on the consequences of his infidelity if word of him and Monica ever got out. *"Pauleena is going to kill me,"*Psycho thought to himself as a loud strong orgasm took control of him.

Chapter Three

H.N.I.C

Dice lay in his king sized water bed shirtless with a remote in his hand. Ever since Wolf had left and put Dice in charge of running The Spades, Dice rarely had time to himself. There was always something going on and someone almost always needed his help or assistance with something. Dice didn't mind spending most of his time solving or helping people with their problems cause at the end of the day that's what he had signed up for. What bothered him was all of the killings. Ever since Pauleena had been locked up it seemed like the murder rate had increased and tripled by three. Word had gotten back to Dice that Pauleena was still calling all the shots from jail. She gave her team the order to kill as many Spades as they could until The Spades were no more. Pauleena's team recruited and supplied any knuckle head willing to put in work with a gun and instructions to shoot a Spade on sight.

Dice made sure that all of the businesses that The Spades owned continued to be run smoothly. He even opened up a few new ones as well. The people in the community loved Dice for his hard work and determination to keep the community a safe place to live and raise a child.

Dice did his best to allow The Spades to patrol and police as many communities as they possibly could with as little violence as possible. That in itself was a task alone.

In the beginning Dice had made sure that The Spades were non-violent and only used violence if necessary, but he quickly changed that law once he saw and realized that Pauleena and her team were playing for keeps. The only way to keep the community safe and peaceful was to fight fire with fire.

On Dice's chest rested Tonya's head. The two were still going strong and doing their best to keep their relationship floating above water, but Dice's new status was becoming a problem and beginning to turn Tonya into an accusing, nagging and complaining type of woman; the worst type of woman to be. It seemed like each and every day she was accusing Dice of cheating on her and lying to her about petty shit. Dice brushed Tonya's jealous ways off and chalked it up to her having a guilty conscious due to all the wrong she had done in her past, but despite the fact he still loved her regardless.

The ringing of Dice's cell phone buzzing loudly on the night stand grabbed his attention as well as caused Tonya to stir awake.

"Yo," Dice answered, as he felt Tonya planting soft kisses on his face. Her breath was hot and the odor was something serious, but he smiled anyway pretending as if the strong odor wasn't as bad as it really was.

"Yo you up?" A newly recruited Spades member named Sonny yelled into the phone.

"Yeah, why wassup?" Dice asked sitting up. By the urgency in Sonny's voice he could tell that more than likely something was wrong.

"Me and The Big Show just arrived at five points," Sonny said speaking in codes. "I think you might want to get down here A. S. A. fucking P."

"I'm on my way." Dice ended the call and went to get out of bed, but Tonya hugged him around his waist denying him access to slip out of the warm bed.

"No baby, I don't want you to go," Tonya whined. "Stay here with me.........pleeeeease."

"I wish I could," Dice said gently removing Tonya's hands from his waist and slipping out the bed.

"But it's dangerous out there," Tonya continued. "And it's freezing."

"I won't be gone too long," Dice countered slipping into his Spades uniform, all black everything. He knew Tonya wasn't worried about how cold it was outside or what danger lied ahead. All she cared about were the women that The Spades attracted and how many of them would be smiling all up in her man's face.

"Why would you want to go out into the cold when you got all this warm, wet pussy sitting right here in this warm bed." Tonya spread her legs apart exposing her hairy pussy. She took two fingers and spread her lips apart doing her best to entice Dice.

"That pussy ain't going nowhere." Dice brushed Tonya's weak attempt to seduce him off as if she was invisible. Dice threw his black hoodie over his head, and then his black leather Pelle jacket over the hoodie, grabbed his 9mm, and kissed Tonya on the forehead.

"Damn, all I get is a forehead kiss?" Tonya crumbled up her face and rolled her eyes.

"Stop acting like that," Dice said before disappearing out the front door.

***

Dice hopped out the back seat of the Black Denali along with three other Spades. Being as though there was a war going on, each Spades member walked with one hand in their pocket or up under their jackets with their fingers on the trigger ready to shoot at will and protect Dice with their lives if need be.

Dice walked up and gave Sonny and The Big Show some dap. "What's goodie?" Dice flicked his wrist and smoothly glanced down at his watch. "It's 3:15 am and freezing out here," he said as if nobody else noticed. "Talk to me."

"Follow me," The Big Sow said as he began leading Dice and the rest of The Spades over towards a low key alley. When Dice and The Spades reached the alley, they immediately looked up and saw three Spades members hanging by their necks from the telephone wires.

"Found them like that almost an hour ago," The Big Show announced. "More and more of ours have been turning up dead."

Dice turned toward one of The Spades standing to his right. "Cut em down," he said through clenched teeth. The sight of three good brothers hanging lifeless from the telephone wires made him sick to his stomach.

"I don't have nothing to cut them down with," the man standing to Dice's right replied.

Before Dice realized it, his hand shot out and smacked the shit out of the man. "Well then go find something to cut them down with!"

"I think it's time to turn it up full throttle on Psycho and the rest of them pussies," The Big Show suggested. He understood that The Spades were out to help clean up the community, but now it was time to start killing as many of them as they could and see which crew would be the last standing. Sitting around waiting to get killed wasn't what The Big Show had signed up for. "I'm tired of just sitting around. It's time to start busting some heads!"

"That's not what Wolf wanted," Dice replied quickly. He knew a lot of The Spades were beginning to get restless and impatient, but he had promised Wolf that he would continue to run The Spades organization the way it was supposed to be ran. All of these killings and going to war wasn't a part of the plan.

"Wolf isn't here anymore," The Big Show pointed out. "And more than likely he won't be coming back."

It was sad to say, but Dice knew that what The Big Show was saying was right. It would be too dangerous and risky for Wolf to return back to New York. That was the main reason Wolf left Dice in charge of running and holding down the operation.

"You gon have to man up and make some grown man decisions," The Big Show said. "Some of the other Spades members are starting to think you're soft and trust me don't nobody want to take orders from a soft nigga," he said truthfully.

"You think I'm soft?" Dice asked looking up at The Big Show.

"It doesn't matter what I think." The Big Show smirked. "It matters how it looks and right now it ain't looking too good."

Dice nodded his head and let The Big Show's words swirl around in his head. At the moment he was stuck in between a rock and a hard place. Dice wanted to continue to clean up and police the community, but adding fuel to the already lit fire was sure to gain the attention of the police. He couldn't save the community and go to war at the same time. It had to be either one or the other.

"Sleep on it tonight and call me tomorrow," The Big Show said and patted Dice on the back as him and Sonny spun off.

Dice stood in the cold waiting for the three Spades members to be cut down from the telephone wires. As he stood there waiting he felt an urgent tap on his shoulder.

"Yo Five- O coming," one of The Spades said quickly. Dice removed the 9mm from his waistband and handed it to the man just as a royal blue Crown Vic pulled up to the curb.

Agent Starks smoothly stepped out the Crown Vic and coolly flipped his collar up so that the cold air wouldn't attack the back of his neck. "You don't look too happy to see me."

"What do you want?" Dice asked dryly.

"You can start by telling me where Wolf is hiding," Agent Starks countered. Agent Starks and Dice continued to exchange words until Agent Starks looked over Dice's shoulder and saw three dead bodies swinging lifelessly from the telephone lines. He whipped his .357 from its holster and pointed it at Dice's face. "Down on the ground now!"

Dice's eyes went from Agent Starks eyes down to the wet, filthy ground. "Nah, you wilding..." He shook his head. "It's too cold out here for all that."

Agent Starks roughly grabbed Dice up and wrestled him down to the wet ground and cuffed him. Five minutes later the entire alley was crawling with police.

***

"So," Agent Starks began as him and Dice's eyes met through the rearview mirror. "The Spades and Pauleena are still going to war huh?"

Dice said nothing.

"The Spades are doing more damage to the city than helping," Agent Starks pointed out. "Ever since The Spades were created the murder rate has risen by the months. All you doing is killing ya own people."

Dice said nothing.

"But guess what?" Agent Starks continued. "If you think I'm just going to sit around and let you stupid ass Spades destroy *my* city then you got another thing coming," he said with his voice raising a few octaves. "You punk motherfuckers wanna keep up with this bullshit and I'm going to have to teach you motherfuckers who the biggest gang in New York City really is."

“Do what you do,” Dice said in an I don’t give a fuck tone. Agent Starks threats didn’t move Dice not one bit. Whatever it was going to be, it was just going to have to be. Whatever happened Dice would make sure that him and The Spades were well prepared for whatever was to come.

Chapter Four

Back Like I Never Left

"Yo who that behind us Five?" Live Wire asked peeking through the rearview mirror as he whipped his all black Camaro through the city. He had shot so many of The Spades and so many of Pauleena's peoples that he felt as if the entire city was out to kill him. The paranoia was getting the best of him, but one thing for sure all this beef had kept Live Wire sharp and on his toes. On his lap sat his .45 sitting over in the passenger seat sat Live Wire's right hand man Bills and on his lap also rested a big hand gun.

Bills craned his neck backwards so he could get a good look. "Nah that ain't nobody," he said squinting his eyes struggling to see out of the heavily dark tint.

"You sure?" Live Wire asked double checking just to be on the safe side. Live Wire's mind was already made up. If *anybody* tried to run up on him there would be shots fired and that went for police too. Live Wire wasn't too worried about The Spades. With Dice running The Spades, The Spades had turned soft. Live Wire was more worried about Pauleena's people. Him and The Real Spades shot and tried to kill any and everybody affiliated with Pauleena. Pauleena had shot Live Wire and in return he had blown her mother's head off, but the two still weren't even. They had some unfinished business to take care of.

Since Pauleena was locked away in jail Psycho called himself wanting to defend his woman's honor. Live Wire gladly accepted the challenge and planned on making an example out of the fake tough guy.

Live Wire quickly pulled into a parking spot in front of a famous soul food restaurant and killed the engine. Standing outside in front of the restaurant stood Sparkle and Bills girlfriend Lisa. They both had angry looks on their faces and rocked from side to side trying to keep warm.

Sparkle sucked her teeth when she spotted the black Camaro pull up in front of the soul food joint. The driver door opened and the sound of Trinidad James song "All Gold Everything" came spilling from the car's speakers at a ridiculous volume. Live Wire and Bills stepped out the car and headed towards the two women that awaited them.

"Hey baby wassup?" Live Wire said leaning in for a kiss, but Sparkle quickly jerked her head back before their lips could connect.

"Hey baby my motherfucking ass!" Sparkle huffed dramatically. She and Lisa had been waiting on Live Wire and Bills for over an hour out in the cold and the two were ready to snap at a drop of a hat. "We been waiting out here for over an hour freezing our asses off," she complained, cutting her eyes at Live Wire.

"Stop putting on a show," Live Wire whispered as he pulled Sparkle in close.

"No," Sparkle said fronting like she wanted Live Wire to release her from his grip. "You always doing this shit, but let me be five minutes late and you'd be ready to rip my head off."

"You acting dumb right now," Live Wire said smoothly. He looked over to his right and noticed that Bills wasn't doing any better with Lisa.

After having to put up with a five minute lecture the foursome finally entered the restaurant.

"Excuse me sir," the hostess said with a polite smile. "Mind removing your hood while you're inside please?"

"You mind, minding ya motherfucking business," Live Wire capped back causing the foursome to erupt with laughter drawing unwanted attention to them as they headed towards an empty booth.

"Come warm my legs up," Sparkle demanded. She wore a sweater that passed for a mini skirt, tights, and black leather boots that came up to her thighs. Whenever she was around Live Wire she tried to look her sexiest and wore as close to nothing as possible.

"So what took y'all so long to get here? What happen, ya'll ran into a couple of ratchet bitches looking to do something strange for a piece of change?" Lisa asked. She was looking to be nosey and start some shit both at the same time.

"There you go," Bills huffed.

"There I go my ass! What the hell took y'all so long?" Lisa pressed the issue hoping to turn this into a debate so all four of them could go back and forth.

"You ask a lot of questions," Live Wire said jumping into the conversation. "Just be happy that we're here. How about that?" He could care less about this non-money conversation. All Live Wire cared about was how he could fatten up his pockets. If Sparkle and Lisa continued on with this dumb shit Live Wire planned on spinning off on the two leaving them in the restaurant alone looking stupid.

"If I was you, I would be quiet," Sparkle said looking at Live Wire like he was crazy. "You already in enough trouble when we get home."

"You promise?" Live Wire smiled as his hand slipped down and palmed Sparkle's huge fake ass.

"I love you Live," Sparkle whispered in Live Wire's ear making sure she ran her tongue across his lobe. "I'm going to swallow that dick whole when we get home." Live Wire may have been a serial cheater and a dope boy, but whatever he was, he belonged to Sparkle and he was all hers. She didn't care what nobody said about *her* man. Sparkle was riding it out with Live Wire until the wheels fell off.

Live Wire answered his ringing cell phone and held up one finger signaling Sparkle to give him one second.

"What you mean?" Live Wire listened to whoever was on his other line spoke, making faces at everything that was said. "Got robbed? By who? How much did they get away with? I'll hit you back."

"What happened?" Bills asked nosily.

Live Wire waited as the waitress sat their plates down on the table, then left before he spoke. "Another one of our spots got hit."

"Say word?" Bills said.

"Word." Live Wire pinched the bridge of his nose. This was the third spot this month that had been robbed. The bad part about it was that Live Wire had no clue who was behind the capers and that's what bothered him the most.

"No word on who's responsible for this shit?" Bills asked ready to kill any and everyone who violated him and The Real Spades.

Live Wire shrugged, "Nah." The news of another one of his spots being robbed had changed his whole mood from chill to angry and violent in a split second.

"I don't mean to be in y'all business or nothing like that." Sparkle said taking a sip of her drink, "But my girl tiffany's man was just robbed and killed not too long ago and she was telling everybody that the Gambino Boys were responsible for robbing and killing her man."

"You mean the Gambino Brother's?" Live Wire corrected her.

"Yeah, yeah the Gambino Brother's that's their name." Sparkle said excitedly. Instantly things went from bad to worse. Live Wire had heard the vicious and violent stories that were linked to the Gambino Brother's name. Two brothers who didn't give a shit about nothing or nobody, but inflicting pain on their victims. The Gambino Brothers were well known throughout the states as being the most ruthless and vicious stick up kids to ever pick up a gun. They had more than enough money to retire and live comfortably for the rest of their lives, but they weren't in it for the money, instead they were in it for the sport which made them ten times more dangerous.

"Who that?" Bills asked confused.

"Two Mexican or Spanish stick up kids that's been terrorizing the streets for years." Live Wire snorted, "But if them motherfuckers think they can rob The Real Spades and get away with it, then they got another thing coming."

"You think it's them?" Bills asked skeptically. "I mean there's a million jack boys and stick up kids running around like cowboys."

At every spot that has been hit several shot gun and .45 shell cases were left behind and everyone know Alex Gambino's weapon of choice is the Mossberg pump shot gun and his brother Victor uses twin .45's. If the GambinoBrothers were in fact behind all of the robberies, Live Wire and The Real Spades planned on teaching them that it wasn't wise to touch a hot stove because you might end up getting burned.

"Who else would be stupid enough to…." Live Wire's words were cut off at the sound of a commotion at the front door of the restaurant that caused the foursome to look that way. A group of women, including several waitresses crowded around the entrance squealing like high school kids while trying to snap pictures or record whoever was coming in the restaurant with their smart phones and tablets.

Snow stormed inside the restaurant like he owned it, like he was the King of the world. His cousin, a knuckle head that went by the name Trouble was with him, flanked by two of his cronies who were draped in jewelry and wore shirts that read the letters M.O.E. on the front. The people eating at the restaurant threw themselves at the feet of the superstar rapper treating him like a god.

The sight of Snow caused Sparkle to get upset; she sucked her teeth, "Yo, that's that motherfucker that put hands on me at The Terminator's party a few months back." She confessed.

Almost a year and a half ago Sparkle attended the number one pound for pound champion of the world, The Terminator's house party and was assaulted by Snow and his entourage because she brushed the rapper off as if he was a nobody and a lame. Snow's entourage didn't like Sparkle's disrespect and violated her by putting hands on her.

"Yo ain't that, that fake rap nigga that always be on World Star?" Bills asked with a smile. He knew shit was getting ready to pop off and he couldn't wait to do bodily harm to the rapper and the members of his entourage.

Instantly Live Wire remembered Snow from the brawl that popped off in the club over a year ago between The Real Spades and Prince and his crew.

"I'm tired of these Bozo's walking around fronting like they really bout that life." Live Wire shot to his feet and headed over towards Snow and his entourage's table with Bills in tow.

"Hold up." Sparkle said as her and Lisa got up and followed their men over towards where Snow and his entourage were seated.

***

Snow sat at the table strolling through his iPhone going back and forth with this new Dominican thing via text message. Snow had so many women that they were all starting to feel the same to him, but this was the life that Snow lived. He was still having trouble dealing with the fact that he was famous now. Snow wanted to continue on living the way he was used to living, but when you're constantly on T.V. your life is always under a microscope and that was the part of being a celebrity Snow was learning and working hard to deal with.

But hanging around Trouble and his M.O.E. (money over everything) crew was turning his transformation into mission impossible.

Lately Snow's mind had been all over the place; he was working on his album, as well as fighting several law suits all at the same time. His M.O.E. crew was still beefing with The Spades and the unnecessary drama was starting to become bad for business. Snow knew if he didn't slow down nobody in the industry would want to deal with or be affiliated with him or his talent. The funny thing about the music business was the more trouble Snow got into, the more his mix tape sold and the more the streets loved him and in result he made more money.

The Dominican woman that Snow had been texting back and forth sent him a few naked pictures of herself.

"Damn shorty shit right." Snow said, passing his cell phone around so everyone at the table could see the Dominican woman's goodies. If it was one thing he loved it was to show off.

"You a foul nigga." Trouble huffed, "You stay cuffing the bad joints."

Before Snow got a chance to reply, two members of his entourage jumped up and restrained a hysterical fan from trying to touch any part of the rapper. Snow sat back and watched as the two members from his entourage struggled and fought to escort the overly excited woman out of the restaurant.

"These bitches been wilding lately." Trouble pointed out. "Following you back to your hotel room, showing up at private parties, you got a few stalkers out there after you." He paused momentarily to take in Snow's reaction and expression to what he was saying. "It may be time for you to invest in some security." Trouble suggested.

"Snow don't do security." Snow replied quickly. In his mind security was for the weak. Any problems that came his way, Snow planned on handling it himself and with extreme force. He kept a bunch of wild ignorant niggaz with him at all times in case something popped off.

"Security is not a bad thing." Trouble said convincingly. "All the rappers got security now a days.

"I ain't like the rest of these fake rap niggaz." Snow boasted. "A nigga try to violate me and I only got two words for him.....hands and feet."

Snow and Trouble's conversation was interrupted when Snow felt a shadow looming over him. "Yo, I ain't giving out autographs right now, come back later." He said in an uninterested tone, not even bothering to look up at the man that stood over him. A quick right hook violently caused Snow's neck to snap back as blood instantly filled his mouth.

Live Wire stole on Snow, and then followed up with a left hook. The second punch drugged Snow as Live Wire snatched the rapper out of the booth by his legs sending him crashing down to the floor awkwardly.

Live Wire looked up and saw Bills and Trouble going blow for blow. The two men spilled out of the booth and went crashing into another couple's table causing loud screams to erupt throughout the restaurant. A few patrons even ran up out the restaurant in fear of their lives and safety.

"Yeah, that's right!" Sparkle cheered from the sideline as she watched Live Wire pound Snow out. "Whip his motherfucking ass!" She was happy to see the cocky rapper get a well-deserved good ass whipping. Sparkle's smile quickly vanished when the two men from Snow's entourage returned from outside and jumped head first in the brawl, turning the brawl from a two on two, to a four on two.

“Oh hell no.” Sparkle rushed and jumped into the fight to help her man. If Live Wire got his ass whipped, then they were both going to get their asses whipped together. There was no way she could sit around and watch her man get jumped and not help him, that’s not how she got down.

Meanwhile Lisa stood on the sideline screaming and calling for help, there was no way she was jumping into the brawl, fighting wasn’t her thing, but if a shit talking competition ever presented itself Lisa would be dead smack in the middle of it.

Lisa watched as Sparkle ran and punched one of Snow’s homeboys on the side of his head, then proceeded to scratch his eyes out. The man wearing the M.O.E. shirt turned and fired a blind punch that landed flush on Sparkle’s chin. The punch didn’t knock Sparkle out, but the impact from the blow put her on her back. The goon went to move in for the kill, but Sparkle kicked her legs wildly making it hard for him to get a hold of her. By this time Live Wire had picked up a chair and crashed it over the goons head.

“Fuck!” Live Wire cursed. He was mad that the cheap chair had broken so easily over the goons head. Live Wire used the broken off piece of wood that remained in his hand to beat the goon half to death for putting his hands on Sparkle.

Several members from the restaurant’s staff ran out from the back and separated the two crews. Snow hopped back up to his feet and swung over the shoulder of an older stocky brother who was holding Live Wire’s back and landed a cheap shot on Live Wire’s chin.

Snow looked around and noticed several people standing around with their cell phones held out recording the entire brawl. Right then and there Snow knew the footage of Live Wire getting the best of him would be uploaded to each and every gossip site’s website within the next hour.

Snow wiped the blood from his mouth. The beating he took wasn’t a good look, but regardless he had no other choice but to hold it down and keep it moving. Live Wire may have gotten the best of him this time, but the next time the two crossed paths Snow planned on clapping something.

"This shit ain't over with motherfucker!" Snow yelled, picked up a chair and tossed it in Live Wire's direction just to save face, and look good for the camera.

The sound of siren's caused both sides to exit the restaurant and head their separate ways. Snow didn't need no more law suits so him and his team fled away from the soul food restaurant, while Live Wire and Bills did the same.

"You want me to drop y'all off at the crib?" Live Wire asked opening the driver door of his Camaro. He gave Lisa a once over and noticed that she was the only one without any bumps or bruises, her clothes still looked fresh like they had just came from the dry cleaners.

"Nah, we gon hop in a cab." Bills said. He was pissed off as well as embarrassed that his shorty didn't jump into the fight to help him out. Thoughts of whipping her ass when they got back home crossed his mind. "I'll text you when I touch down."

"You sure?" Live Wire asked. He could tell that something was bothering Bills.

"Yeah, I'm good." Bills flashed a fake smile.

"Come on baby, let's catch this cab and hurry up and get home *we* had a rough night." Lisa said looping her arm around Bills arm.

Bills snatched his arm out of her grip. "Yeah, bitch *we* did have a rough night. *We* meaning, me, Live Wire, and Sparkle. You," He jabbed his finger in Lisa's face. "Had an easy night!"

"What!?" Lisa crumbled up her face. "I wasn't jumping in that fight, plus I just got my nails done." She said like that explained everything. "I don't know what kind of ratchet bitches you used to dealing with, but I ain't one of them, if you want a hood rat then I suggest you go to the gutter and find one, cause I don't do ratchet." She said in a matter of fact tone.

"I'm sorry baby; I'm just a little upset right now." Bills said in a calm tone. He grabbed Lisa's hand and kissed her fingertips lovingly. "You forgive me?" Without warning Bills turned and head butted Lisa, he followed up with an uppercut to the stomach causing her to drop down to her hands and knees.

Bills raised his boot and stomped down on Lisa's fingertips. "Fuck them stupid ass nails bitch!" He cleared his throat and spat a glob of phlegm in Lisa's freshly done weave.

"She just got her nails done." Bills repeated out loud shaking his head walking aimlessly down the street.

Live Wire walked over to Lisa like he was about to help her out, then swiftly raised his boot and stomped down on Lisa's other hand. "Ya nails was whack anyway bitch." He laughed loudly, hopped behind the wheel of his Camaro and pulled off.

For the entire ride back home Sparkle and Live Wire laughed and joked about the fight that took place at the restaurant.

"I know that clown Snow gon be tight when the whole world sees the footage of him getting fucked up." Sparkle laughed as her and Live Wire entered their mini mansion. Sparkle noticed that only the bottom lock on the door was locked and she clearly remembered locking both the top and bottom lock. Just as Sparkle was about to bring the news to Live Wire's attention she felt a pair of soft lips kissing down her neck.

"Thank you for holding ya man down." Live Wire said in between kisses as he darted his tongue in and out of Sparkle's mouth.

"You...know I'll...ride...or die...for you." Sparkle moaned in between kisses. In a quick motion Live Wire pulled Sparkle's sweater/skirt over her head and began sucking on her plus sized titties. Instantly the treasure between Sparkle's legs became wet.....real wet. Live Wire effortlessly lifted Sparkle up and sat her down on top of the marble counter top; he then aggressively ripped the stockings around the crotch area. A smile appeared on Live Wire's face when he found out that Sparkle didn't have on no panties.

"I don't do draws." Sparkle growled as if she was reading Live Wire's mind. Live Wire laid Sparkle down on the counter; she was naked except for the tights and mid thigh high black leather boots that were still on her feet. Live Wire pinned Sparkle's legs all the way back to her head, looked down and saw a fresh waxed, fat, wet pussy staring up at him.

"I missed you." Live Wire said talking to the pussy. He dipped his head in between Sparkle's thick thighs and gave her pussy a nice slow tongue kiss. Immediately Sparkle's legs tensed, her breathing did the same. She grabbed Live Wire's head, shifted her hips towards his face and released a slow, long moan. She made curt sounds like mmm and ahhh along with a bunch of other animal type of noises. The sound of Live Wire's mouth was real wet, loud and nasty, his tongue was on a mission and determined to force Sparkle to cum in his mouth.

Sparkle moaned, she moaned deep, her body shaking, her hands holding Live Wire's face, pulling him deeper into her vagina, getting turned on by the slurping that came from between her legs. "Yes Daddy!" She moaned. "That's right suck on that pussy!" Her legs locked around Live Wire's neck, the feeling was so good that Sparkle didn't want it to end. "Damn you bout to make a bitch cum in your mouth." She growled through clinched teeth. "You want me to cum in your mouth Daddy? Huh? That's what you want? That's what you want?" Sparkle panted as her breathing went from smooth to choppy. "That's right Daddy eat this pussy like you mean it, I swear this pussy is all yours, I swear it’s all yours." Sparkle moaned grinding her pussy even further on Live Wire's face. Moans that started off soft now became desperate. The more noises Sparkle made, the louder Live Wire slurped and sucked on her swollen clit, his tongue worked over time as he went all out to please his woman.

Sparkle was sweating as if she was suffering. Her entire body tensed, her toes curled inside her boots, her nails raked Live Wire's flesh. "Yes, yes, yes, oh shit, oh my fucking god, yes Daddy!" Sparkle screamed, then closed her eyes like she was praying, she jerked, tightened her thighs around Live Wire's neck moaned like the devil was inside of her fighting for freedom, then released a hard, strong, powerful orgasm that left her body shaking and trembling.

Live Wire stood up, wiped his mouth with the back of his hand and smiled. He loved pleasing Sparkle, he thought it was hilarious how every time after a sex session Sparkle acted as if she couldn't move and was frozen for a few moments. Live Wire fixed his mouth to clown Sparkle, but an angry voice grabbed his attention.

"You a nasty motherfucker!"

Live Wire spun around to see the face of the man that the voice belonged to. Victor Gambino stood a few feet away from Live Wire with a .45 in both hands, he kept one trained on Live Wire and the other aimed at Sparkle. "When did it become cool to eat a prostitute's pussy?"

"Watch ya mouth." Live Wire capped back.

"Or else what?" Alex Gambino appeared behind Live Wire and Sparkle; he dramatically cocked a round into his shot gun with the pistol grip. Word on the streets was that Live Wire and The Real Spades were getting a lot of money and The Gambino Brother's wanted in and dared for Live Wire or anyone for that matter to tell them no.

Sparkle hopped down off the counter, her heels making a loud clank when her feet hit the floor. She looked at the pillow case filled with what she assumed was the money that was in Live Wire's safe that dangled in Alex's hand. "You got the money, now why don't you two get back on the banana boat that y'all floated in on and bounce?" She disrespected with a smirk on her face. That smirk was instantly wiped off of her face when her head violently jerked back, from being hit with one of Victor Gambino's .45's. Sparkle's mouth filled with blood as she spit one of her front teeth out into the palm of her hand and started crying like a baby. She looked over at Live Wire silently asking him to defend her and retaliate.

"What do you two wet backs want from me?" Live Wire asked in a bored tone. He had been caught slipping and figured he was as good as dead. Knowing the Gambino Brother's reputation, he figured his life was on a countdown.

"We're looking for Live Wire." Alex moved next to his brother Victor and aimed his shot gun at Live Wire's stomach.

"Look no further, you've found him." Live Wire replied. He was a little scared, but wouldn't dare let his emotions show on his face. "What do you two clowns want from me?"

"The organization known as The Spades." Alex said in an even tone. "You are one of the leaders no?"

"Nah, I don't fuck with The Spades." Live Wire confessed. "Me and my peoples are going to war with The Spades as we speak."

"So you have no affiliation with The Spades?" Alex asked with a raised brow. The Spades were out trying to rid the streets of all of the drugs dealers and The Gambino Brothers couldn't just sit back and allow that to happen. If there were no drug dealers then that meant the Gambino Brother's couldn't eat and there was no way the Gambino Brothers were going to let The Spades or anyone for that matter stop them from eating.

Live Wire shook his head. "I don't fuck with them bird ass niggaz no more."

"I was told two men that went by the names of Wolf and Live Wire were The Spades leaders." Alex said raising the shot gun up to Live Wire's head.

"I think I need an ambulance." Sparkle mumbled looking at Live Wire, holding her bloody mouth.

Live Wire ignored Sparkle and continued his conversation with the Gambino Brother's.

"I was one of The Spades leaders once upon a time, but of course times have changed." He leaned coolly back up against the counter.

"So who the fuck are the leaders then?" Victor barked. His patience had run out as soon as he had stepped foot inside the house and he was getting ready to empty a clip in something. He wasn't with all this talking shit.

"Wolf, and Dice." Live Wire told him. "Wolf has been M.I.A. for a while, so Dice is the man you're looking for."

Alex nodded. "Thank you for your time and sorry for any trouble we may of caused you." He looked over at Sparkle who was still holding her bloody mouth and crying.

"Fuck you mean sorry?" Live Wire crumbled up his face. "You come in here, take all my money, pistol whip my bitch and you think by you saying sorry is going to fix that?"

"Sorry is the best I can do, if that ain't good enough, catch us in the streets." Alex smiled, "The Gambino Brother's ain't hard to find."

"Will do." Live Wire said as he watched the Gambino Brother's make their exit.

Chapter Five

You In or Out

Agent Starks walked through the F.B.I. Headquarters with a serious look on his face. The wrinkled brown suit he wore announced that it had been a while since he had slept, bathed or even changed clothes. Agent Starks was a dedicated Agent and one of the best Agents out there and the words sleep, stop, can't or slow down weren't in his vocabulary. The war between Pauleena, The Spades and The Real Spades was beginning to get out of control and it was Agent Starks job to put an end to the madness by any means necessary.

He reached his Lieutenant's office and gave the wooden door a light knock.

"Come in!" A rough sounding voice ordered from the other side of the door. Agent Starks entered the office and spotted his Lieutenant along with a beautiful Honey Brown skin woman who had plenty of sex appeal. On her feet were some to die for heels that agent Starks imagined hurt her feet.

"Agent Starks so glad you could join us." Lieutenant said with a smile that said he was up to no good. "Please have a seat." He motioned towards the vacant chair that sat a few feet away from the attractive woman with the hot shoes. Once agent Starks sat down the Lieutenant began. "As you know this stupid ass war that's been going on between Pauleena, the spades, and the real spades is no good." He stared at Agent Starks. "I'm going to need you to work overtime and personally put an end to this."

"What exactly are you saying?" Agent Starks asked wanting to be clear. He wasn't the type that liked to talk in riddles.

The Lieutenant leaned in closer and lowered his tone. "What I'm saying is *you* are going to put an end to this stupid ass war." He smiled "We not playing or pussy footing around with these animals no more! They want to run around and kill each other like animals then we're going to have to slaughter them like animals."

"Sir, I'm out here doing the best I can, but…"

"I have a thirty man team of killers with badges." The Lieutenant said cutting Agent Starks off as if what he was saying wasn't important or worth listening to. "It's time to start fighting fire with fire....you go out and find as many of Pauleena's peoples, spades, and Real Spades and I want you to kill them!"

The Lieutenants words caught Agent Starks off guard. He wasn't expecting to hear this when he walked into the office. To go out and just start killing people would make agent Starks no better than the rest of the animals he tried so hard to capture and locked away every day and that was something he wasn't sure he could live with. "Lieutenant I'm not so sure that's a good idea."

"It's a great idea and the only option." The Lieutenant said in a matter of fact tone. "We kill these animals and that's the end of this pointless ass war and the murder rate will decrease." He paused. "Think about how many lives we'd be saving… We'll be saving lives and getting rid of the city's most reckless and arrogant killers." The Lieutenant continued, "Aren't you tired of building these long cases on these guys just to have their hot shot lawyers come and get them a slap on the wrist? Huh?"

Everything that the Lieutenant was saying was right, but Agent Starks wasn't sure if he wanted anything to do with the mission at hand. Going out to flat out murder someone, no matter who it was, was wrong.

"Sir, can we talk about this another time, when we have a little more privacy?" Agent Starks said nodding towards the attractive woman who sat next to him. He wasn't too comfortable talking about a matter of this magnitude in front of a total stranger.

"Please forgive me, where are my manners?" The Lieutenant chuckled. "Agent Starks I'd like for you to meet Agent Smith, Agent Smith, Agent Starks." He introduced the two.

"Mind telling me what she's doing here?" Agent Starks asked with a suspiciously raised brow.

"Certainly." The Lieutenant became serious again. "While you're out *cleaning* up the streets, Agent Smith will be in the fields working undercover." He paused again. "She's going undercover into the federal prison to help bring down Pauleena, from what I hear Pauleena has been having some problems while in prison with a few of the Spades so I'm guessing that soon she'll fly off the handle and kill one of the women in the prison and were going to need a witness, inside Agent Smith here is going to get close to Ms. Diaz and see if she can get her to admit to a murder or anything that we can use to add more time onto her sentence."

Agent Starks massaged his temples. "Are you trying to get this woman killed? Pauleena will see right through this bullshit..." He turned his gaze on the attractive woman. "No offense Agent Smith, but maybe you should try an assignment that's a little less challenging."

"And maybe you should grow some nuts and stop juggling them." Agent Smith capped back with much attitude.

"Juggling them?" Agent Starks repeated confused.

"Yeah, in your mouth." She said slyly. Agent Smith had clearly violated her fellow agent, but she could give two fucks about the coward that sat next to her. "I'm the only female agent with enough heart to step up and accept this assignment." Agent Smith boasted. "Besides I'm overqualified for the mission at hand, I grew up in the projects, so prison can't be too much worse."

"You do know that Pauleena still has two years left on her sentence?" Agent Starks informed Agent Smith. "You're willing to spend twenty-four months in a woman's federal prison?Huh?"

"It won't take me 24 months to gather up enough evidence to put Ms. Diaz away for the rest of her life." Agent Smith stated; her tone full of arrogance. She was the best female agent in the department and looked forward to the challenge of trying to take down the infamous Pauleena. "If I didn't think I can handle the assignment I wouldn't have accepted it."

Agent Starks gave the arrogant agent a sad look. "Good luck." He knew that Agent Smith was in over her head, but some people just had to learn the hard way and unfortunately Agent Smith was one of those type of people, she had already signed her death certificate, all Agent Starks could do now was pray for her.

"I won't need it, but thanks anyway." Agent Smith flashed a beautiful smile.

"When does her mission start?"

"Tomorrow morning." The Lieutenant answered.

"What's going to be her undercover name?" Agent Starks asked.

"Remy" Agent Smith answered, as she stood to her feet. "It was nice meeting you… nah, I'm lying." She laughed, said goodbye to the Lieutenant, then made her exit out of the office.

All the Lieutenant could do was shake his head. Agent Smith was a little feisty and rough around the edges, but those attributes were just what was going to help her in bringing down Pauleena. It was a shot in the dark, but at the end of the day it was only shot in.

Chapter Six

You Got Me

"Keep your hands above the table, if you're going to kiss, kiss but no making out. If you need to use the bathroom you raise your hand first. Myself or another officer will let you know if you are *allowed* to use it or not." A short round blue eyed C.O. chick said looking at Pauleena like she was better than her because she had her freedom and Pauleena didn't. "You understand what I just told you?"

"Yeah, yeah, yeah." Pauleena huffed. "I understand."

The C.O. jumped in Pauleena's face like she was the gangsta in prison and Pauleena was the citizen at work. "Let me tell you something Diaz I'm the last person in the world that you want to piss off."

"Its better to be pissed off then pissed on." Pauleena countered not backing down. She couldn't stand the racist police bitches at the prison and made it a point to give them a hard time every chance she got.

"I'll deal with you later." The C.O. growled and gave Pauleena a light shove in her back. To the average person the little shove may not have looked like much, but the Pauleena the C.O. had just crossed the line and she planned on dealing with her at a later time, right now she had a visit to attend to.

After getting patted down Pauleena was allowed to enter the visiting room. The visiting room was filled with loud chatter, laughing and crying babies. Pauleena's eyes scanned the entire visiting room until she spotted psycho sitting at a table over in the cut, the closer Pauleena got to psycho she noticed that his table was filled with all kinds of snacks.

"Hey baaaaby!" Pauleena squealed as she jumped up in her man's arms. It felt good be back in Psycho's arms. She grabbed psycho's face and kissed him like he was the last man on earth. Their tongue danced a slow unhurried dance. They kissed endlessly, Psycho's hands moved down to Pauleena' s breast, touched the right one, then his finger circled the nipple on the right. Pauleena shifted in his naughtiness. Psycho's hand moved down Pauleena's body and settled on her tight plump ass.

"I've been missing you like crazy." Psycho whisper in Pauleena's ear as he looked up and noticed all the C.O.'s staring at him giving him dirty and nasty look.

It disgusted the correctional officers to see inmates family and loved ones visit them or show them any type of love. Once the two were seated Pauleena began. "How things been on the other side?"

"Money still rolling in." Psycho replied. "Still no sign of Wolf."

"Wolf is such a pussy." Pauleena said as if just saying his name disgusted her. "Ran into a few Spade bitches in here." She smiled. "Bitches tried to style on me."

"Word?"

"Word, but I held it down."

"You better start working out while you in here." Psycho told her. Deep down inside Psycho was worried about Pauleena's safety while she was in prison. Things ran totally different in prison than they did in the streets, there was nowhere to hide or run. You have to see the same people day in and day out whether you wanted to or not.

"Start working out." Pauleena looked at Psycho like he was crazy. "Working out ain't gonna help me dodge a bullet."

All psycho could do was laugh at how stubborn his woman was, no matter what Pauleena was just going to be Pauleena. "You still want to get married when you get out? I know things didn't turn out too good last time we tried to tie the knot." Psycho chuckled as he thought back to the big shootout between them and the Spades, in the middle of the ceremony.

"That all depends on you." Pauleena said turning dead serious. "You've been keeping in your dick in your pants since I've been gone?"

Immediately psycho's mind thought about his side chick Monica on the nasty things that they been doing behind closed doors since Pauleena had been shipped off to jail. Shame and guilt flushed through his body as he did his best not to let his emotions show on his face. "Of course I have been you know I wouldn't violate you like that, especially while you're in *here*." He lied with a straight face. "You *know* me better than that."

"Don't make me have to hurt nobody when I get out of here." Pauleena spat. She was staring Psycho in his eyes looking for any trace of anything that wasn't authentic. She wanted to trust Psycho, but she knew how much temptation was out here and she also knew how trifling women could be.

"You always wanna hurt a bitch." Psycho chuckled and shook his head.

"I ain't talking about hurting no bitch; I'm talking about hurting you." Pauleena said seriously. "Please don't make me hurt you Psycho… Please."

Pauleena's words wiped the smile right off of Psycho's face. He knew Pauleena was serious that's why he went above and beyond to keep him and Monica's relationship as quiet and low key as possible.

Psycho scooted in his chair closer to Pauleena and dipped his hand under the table. "What I told you about talking stupid while you in here?" He reached up under the table and discreetly touched Pauleena's exposed pussy. The night before

Pauleena used her nail clipper to cut a hole in her khaki pants in between her legs, so that if she was standing the hole couldn't be seen by the correctional officers. Psycho had already given the order not to wear any panties.

"What I told you about talking stupid?" Psycho growled as he played with Pauleena's swollen clit under the table. His fingers instantly became drenched in Pauleena's juices. Pauleena jerked and shifted as soft low moans escaped her lips. She hadn't been touched by a man in so long that as soon as Psycho touched her sex she felt like she was ready to cum, ready to cream in her man's hands right there in the visiting room. "Didn't I tell you, you have to trust me?" Psycho moved his fingers in a quick circular motion. "Huh? You in jail now you don't trust your Daddy no more?"

"I'm sorry Daddy." Pauleena moaned with her eyes shut tight, she wanted to gyrate her hips so bad, wanted to ride his fingers, wanted to feel those same fingers sliding in and out of her, but knew she had to restrain herself from doing such not wanting to bring any unwanted attention her way.

"What?"

"I said I'm...sorry...Daddy." Pauleena moaned, spreading her legs open even wider as a thousand little deaths approached her, her orgasm building like a stack of *Lego's*.

"You been missing your Daddy?" Psycho asked in a sexually charged voice, his fingers sped up moving like they were controlled by batteries. "This my pussy? Huh? Huh?" his fingers moved even faster. "Huh? I can't hear you." He continued to torture her. Watching her moan and squirm only excited Psycho even more.

"This is *all* your pussy." Pauleena moaned as her orgasm arrived like a determined storm, consumed her, devastated her and left her tingling from her forehead down to her toes.

Psycho removed his hands from under the table, looked over both shoulders, then slipped his wet fingers into his mouth and sucked them clean, looked up at Pauleena and flashed a devilish smile. "I love you."

"No, I love you." Pauleena said placing soft kisses on Psycho's hands. Jail wasn't shit to Pauleena; she had been through way worse. Having your freedom taken away from you and being placed in a prison was all a mental thing. One had to be mentally strong to survive. The time wasn't what bothered Pauleena, she could do the time standing on her head if she had too, what bothered her the most was being away from Psycho. She missed everything about him, from the biggest down to the smallest of things. Pauleena knew she had a good man, but not being able to touch or be around her man whenever she wanted to, plus the fact that a bitch was always lurking added on to Pauleena's jealousy and had her thinking all kinds of shit. "I know I be bugging sometimes, I just love you so much and I'll lose my mind if I find out that you out there giving *my* dick away."

"Being in jail got you bugging right now." Psycho told her. "I be so busy out in them streets I don't even have time for no bitches."

"I spoke to my counselor the other day." Pauleena changed the subject, no longer wanting to think about her man giving what was *hers* away. "And she told me with good behavior I can be out of her in twelve months." She smiled.

"Say word."

Pauleena smiled. "Word." She knew the news of her being released early would put a smile on Psycho's face. "Don't tell nobody though, I don't want nobody to know that I'm getting out I just want to pop up on motherfuckers, you know."

Psycho nodded his head. "You already know, you just make sure you keep your nose clean while you in here, I know you gotta do what you gotta do, just make sure you put some shade on it."

Without warning a husky C.O. walked over and knocked on the table loudly. "Visiting hours are over!"

"I can't stand these motherfuckers." Pauleena spat. She stood to her feet and melted in Psycho's arms. His arms felt like the safest place in the world to be at the moment and she didn't want the moment to end.

"Twelve more months and all this shit will be all over with." Psycho assured her. "And when those gates open I promise I'll be on the other side waiting for you. No matter what."

"No matter what." Pauleena tongued Psycho down, got a few cheap feels, then headed towards the back where she was stripped searched. The C.O. with the nasty attitude and blue eyes had the pleasure of searching Pauleena.

"Hand me your shirt." The C.O. ordered with a smirk on her face. Pauleena removed her shirt and handed it to the C.O.

"Boots."

Pauleena removed her boots and handed them to the C.O. she watched as the C.O. searched through her boots like she had a gun hidden inside them.

"Pants."

Pauleena removed her pants and handed them to the C.O. The C.O. snatched Pauleena's pants from her hand and immediately her eyes went down to Pauleena's bush. "Where the fuck are your panties?"

"I don't do panties." Pauleena cracked a smile. She hated being searched after a visit. This seemed to be the best part of the dike C.O.'s job, especially when a beauty like Pauleena showed up.

"You reckless eye balling me!?" The C.O. took her forearm and shoved it up under Pauleena's chin and forced her backwards until Pauleena's back made contact with the wall. "This is my last time warning you Diaz. You don't want to get on my bad side."

Pauleena's nose flared, but she remained silent. *"Twelve more months."*She kept repeating over and over in her head, all she had to do was survive for twelve more months.

"You may be a killer when you on the streets, but in here you ain't shit but a number." The C.O. growled. "Now bend over and spread em."

***

Back on the gallery Pauleena walked down the tier and as usual it was noisy and loud. As she walked down the tier she glanced inside a few cells and saw a few girls playing chess, another girl braiding another girl's hair and a few other inmates sitting around talking shit. Just as Pauleena reached her cell she spotted Jessica the chick who had taken her Tatar tots, then jumped over the table and caught her with a cheap shot in the mess hall walking towards the shower room. Pauleena quickly glanced down at Jessica's feet and noticed that the woman was wearing a pair of shower shoes, a big no, no in prison especially when you were banging and had beef. Pauleena slipped in her cell and stopped in mid-stride. In front of her stood a honey skinned chick unpacking her things placing them on the top bunk. A new bunky, Just what Pauleena needed another nosey bitch all up in her space.

"Hey." The bunky said when she noticed Pauleena standing there.

"Hey." Pauleena said dryly, stepping over the girls draft bags.

"Remy." The girl said introducing herself.

"Pauleena." Pauleena replied as she sat on her bunk, grabbed a sock and began loading the sock with several cans of tuna fish.

"You mind if I sit my bag here for a second?" Remy asked. Seeing Pauleena up close and in person and being alone in a cell with her was a totally different story from reading over her files at a desk.

"I don't give a fuck what you do, just stay out my way and we won't have no problems." Pauleena said removing her shirt. She stood in a sports bra, tan khakis and a pair of black Uggs covered her feet.

For a second Remy though about hitting Pauleena with a slick come backline, but glanced down at the sock filled with cans of tuna fish and thought better of it. From the look on Pauleena' s face Remy could tell that something was about to pop off, she was trained to read body language and right now Pauleena' s body language said to stay the fuck out of her way.

"Pardon self." Pauleena brushed past Remy, slipped the loaded sock down into her back pocket, then headed straight for the shower room. She was on a mission and refused to be denied.

Pauleena entered the shower room and grabbed some scrawny looking white girl who was drying off and tossed her out of the shower room, then slammed the door behind her. Instantly Jessica looked up and saw Pauleena standing in the shower room fully dressed. Right then and there Jessica already knew what time it was.

"Oh I see you one of them hard headed bitches." Jessica spat. She stood talking to Pauleena as if she wasn't butt naked. Jessica was a big girl, but she wasn't fat nor was she skinny. Jessica rinsed the remaining soap suds off of her body, then cut the shower off, as she noticed Pauleena heading towards her. All the steam that filled the shower room and floated through the air made it hard for Jessica or Pauleena to see clearly. "Come on bitch." Jessica growled taking a defensive stance. Once Pauleena was within arm reach, Jessica fired off a quick jab.

Pauleena weaved the jab and caught Jessica with a stiff right hook. Jessica's head snapped back as the strap on her shower slippers broke off. Once Pauleena saw Jessica struggling to keep her footing she went in for the kill and fired punches from all angles hitting Jessica all in her face and head. Jessica fought back as best she could, but every time she tried to gain momentum in the fight Pauleena hit her with another punch.

Jessica kicked off her other shower shoe, backed up and took a second to regroup. She eyed Pauleena closely, the fresh scratches that covered her face were beginning to burn and sting, so she quickly moved on to plan B. Jessica charged Pauleena and was rewarded with two stiff punches to the face. Jessica took the punches well, reached out and grabbed a handful of Pauleena hair. "Bitch!" Jessica barked, then tossed Pauleena into the wall by her hair. Pauleena's body sounded off loudly when it made contact with the wall. Jessica held Pauleena's hair with one hand and fired off several punches to her face, followed by a few knee strikes.

Outside the shower room Remy as well as several other inmates stood outside the shower room's door listening to the gruesome battle that was taking place on the other side of the door. They didn't know what was going on, but from the sound of it they could tell that it was going down.

"Talk that shit now!" Jessica growled. She took Pauleena's head and banged it against the wall. She outweighed and over powered Pauleena and was using her weight, size and power to her advantage. Jessica stayed close to Pauleena, stayed on the inside making it hard for Pauleena to get a punch off.

Jessica and Pauleena tussled, tossing each other against the wet walls in the shower room. Jessica went to throw a powerful uppercut, but lost her footing on the slippery floor, in mid swing and fell down on her knees. This was just the opportunity that Pauleena had been waiting for. She swiftly removed the loaded sock from her back pocket and swing it like it was a pair of nun chucks. The cans inside the sock clanked loudly when it made contact with Jessica's forehead. Instantly a huge gash opened up right above Jessica's eyes.

Pauleena smiled when she saw the scared, dazed and hurt look in Jessica's eyes. "Bitch didn't I tell you I was the wrong one to fuck with!?" Pauleena swung the loaded sock repeatedly beating Jessica into a bloody pulp. "I'mma teach...you...bum ass bitches...about fucking....with a boss bitch!" Pauleena yelled as her arm finally got tired from swinging the sock. She looked down at Jessica's unconscious body and gave her face one last stomp. "Bum ass bitch" Pauleena spat on Jessica, walked over to the shower and turned it on, then exited the shower room. She stepped out the shower room and noticed several other inmates giving for funny looks as she walked down the tier with specs of blood decorating her face, neck, hair and clothes.

Everyone in the jail knew that you didn't fuck with The Spades, that was like committing suicide. The Spades were deep, promoted violence and ready to go at a drop of a hat.

An older inmate approached Pauleena with a sad look on her face. "I'm going to pray for you sister." was all she said, then walked off.

Chapter Seven

Drama Season

Wolf sat on the suede couch in the one bedroom apartment sipping on Ciroc and Pineapple juice. He chose a one bedroom low income apartment in the hood for him and Ivy to crash at in hopes of flying under the radar. He was still a wanted man and had to move like Bin Laden, so he figured what better place to lay low at then the hood, at least he wouldn't stick out like a sore thumb. The adjustment from New York to Los Angeles was a rough one for Wolf; he was used to that fast New York life. Los Angeles was a fast city as well, just a different type of fast and not the type of fast that Wolf was used too.

Going from living in a mansion to a one bedroom apartment was beginning to fuck with Wolf's head, he was beginning to catch himself fussing and complaining about every little thing. To go from living like a king one day then the next day to living like a peasant was a major transition that Wolf was still trying to adjust to. Ivy on the other hand was more happy than she had ever been in her life. The big house, money and cars didn't mean nothing to Ivy she'd gladly go without all of those things if in return she could spend the rest of her life with Wolf.

Ivy was just glad and thankful that Wolf had made it out of New York alive, in one piece and with his freedom, she didn't care if she had to work two jobs to take care of and support them, wait on tables, scrub floors, flip burgers it didn't matter, if that meant her and Wolf would be together then she would do all of those things with a smile and her head held high.

Wolf sat on the couch waiting B.E.T. getting his sip on when he heard Ivy come out for the bathroom with her hands behind her back and a smile on her face. "Guess what?" She beamed.

"We moving back to New York?"

Ivy shook her head. "Nope, try again."

"You finally agree we should move into a bigger house." Wolf said dryly. Not being able to help people and being locked up in the crib all day, every day was beginning to kill his spirit.

"Must you sound so dry?" Ivy leaned down and planted a soft wet kiss in the center of his forehead. "Is there anything I can do to put a smile on that handsome face of yours?" She asked showing all of her thirty two teeth.

Wolf couldn't understand what Ivy was so happy about, their living conditions were fucked up, the neighborhood they lived in was fucked up and at the moment Wolf felt as if their lives were fucked up.

"How bout we move to a nicer house for starters."

"We don't want to attract too much attention, plus you don't want to live too close to them crackers you know they stay watching the news and it'll be just our luck that one of them recognize you and turn you in to the police." Ivy pointed out.

"You act like niggaz don't want the news just as much, besides it's the *black* people that's running around here switching and telling on each other." Wolf grouched.

"Okay, what's the problem?" Ivy asked standing directly in front of the T.V. so she could have Wolf's undivided attention. "I'm tired of seeing you moping around like a zombie...what's *really* the problem?"

"This crib is too small."

"But a jail cell is much smaller." Ivy countered. "You need to count your blessings instead of only pointing out all the negative...try it, it might make you smile a little more."

Wolf flashed a fake smile. He was sick and tired of sitting around the house all day hearing gun shots, police sirens and witnessing a whole bunch of drug dealing going on right up under his nose and not do nothing about it, he was still a Spade at heart and was itching to begin the process of trying to clean up the hoods in L.A., but he knew that was something Ivy wouldn't approve of so he did his best to scratch the idea from his brain.

"You give up?" Ivy sang snapping Wolf out of his thoughts.

"Huh?"

"I asked you to guess what." Ivy smiled. "You give up?"

"I give up." Wolf conceded.

"Surprise!" Ivy sang and showed Wolf a pregnancy test stick that revealed positive results. "*We're* having a baby!"

just by the look on Ivy's face he could tell that she was super excited, so he placed a smile on his face and faked excitement, if they were going to have a baby he damn sure didn't plan on bringing a baby into the world living in a crappy one bedroom apartment in a drug and gang infested neighborhood, but Wolf decided to save that conversation for another day.

"What's wrong?" Ivy asked sensing that something was wrong. "Are you not excited?"

Wolf pulled Ivy down onto his lap and gave her a slow wet sloppy tongue kiss. "Of course I'm excited baby. You said we can talk about anything right?"

"Of course we can." Ivy said with a smile, but on the inside she was preparing herself for something bad.

"I don't know how to say this."

"Just say it!" Ivy said with more aggression in her tone than she intended on using.

"I just want to tell you that I promise I'm going to be the best father in the whole wide world!" Wolf said finally showing excitement.

"Boy!" Ivy punched him in his arm. "You had me scared to death."

"Shut up." Wolf kissed Ivy again. "You know you are my everything."

"Mmmhmm yeah I'm everything until this baby is born, then you going to start treating me like a used condom." Ivy joked, then hopped up off of Wolf's lap.

"Never."

"Come with me to the supermarket so I can grab a few things and cook us a nice dinner so we can celebrate." Ivy said excitedly.

"It's quiet." Wolf said lazily, he was chilling and didn't feel like going outside and he damn sure didn't feel like going to no supermarket.

Ivy plucked Wolf's cup of liquor out of his hand. "If you come with me to the supermarket I promise I'll make it worth your while when we get back."

"You see that's how you got pregnant in the first place." Wolf laughed. He was madly in love with Ivy, the only thing that scared him was the fear of hurting or disappointing her. She was a good girl, not perfect but still good enough to put a ring on her finger and move all the way to another coast for her.

Wolf made an aggravated noise in the process of peeling himself off the couch. "Yo listen, don't be up in the supermarket all day looking at every little thing either." he huffed. "Get what you need, so we can go."

"Yes Daddy." Ivy sang sexily. She knew Wolf didn't really like going to the supermarket, but for her Ivy knew there wasn't nothing that Wolf wouldn't do to keep a smile on her face. Wolf and Ivy stepped foot out of their apartment and noticed that the hood was live and full of movement and activity.

As Wolf walked over towards Ivy's Kia he glanced over to his right and saw a group of men leaning up against a car sipping 40 ounces, trying to disguise the beer in brown paper bags.

"Motherfuckers still drinking 40's" Wolf said to himself as he noticed another group of men huddles up in a circle rolling dice. Women walked up and down the street in pajamas, house shoes and scarves on their heads. Over to his left Wolf noticed two chicks sitting on the stoop, in between their legs rested two men getting their hair braided, in one apartment the door was left open and the voice of "Snoop Dog" could be heard blasting from the apartment, little children ran up and down the streets unattended. The neighborhood looked like the hood in a movie, "Training Day." and everything about the entire situation disgusted Wolf.

"I know this isn't the best of neighborhoods, but just know that it's only temporary." Ivy said as if she could read Wolf's mind. She knew that all the negative activity disgusted Wolf. As Ivy pulled out the parking spot she witnessed several drug transactions take place right out in the open in broad daylight. Just from looking at the people in the neighborhood Ivy could tell that they were unintelligent, ignorant and ratchet.

"And I thought New York was bad." Wolf said. "I should have started The Spades out here."

Ivy turned and gave Wolf an ugly look. "I thought we talked about this already?"

"What you talking about?"

"You can't save and help everybody baby. People are only going to change when they're ready to change." Ivy told him.

"I didn't say nothing about helping or saving nobody."

"But you were thinking it." Ivy countered.

"How you know what I'm thinking?"

"I just do." Ivy smiled.

Wolf shook his head, "now niggaz is mind readers."

"All I'm saying is.........."

"Yo, watch out!" Wolf shouted. Immediately Ivy stomped down on the brakes bringing the car to an abrupt stop.

Ivy looked up and saw a little girl who couldn't have been no older than three or four year's old standing in the middle of the street a few feet away from her car. If Wolf wasn't on point Ivy would have run the little girl over and killed her by accident. "Oh my god!" Ivy held her chest knowing how close she had come to taking an innocent child's life.

Wolf slid out the passenger seat and went to go check on the little girl. "Yo you aight?" Wolf bent down and asked the little girl. The little girl didn't reply. She was a cute little girl, but her hair wasn't done, her face was dirty and her nose was running, the sight and conditions the little girl was living in pissed Wolf off. No child should *ever* have to live like that.

"Do you know where you live?" Wolf asked the little girl.

"One dollar." The little girl said with her hand held out.

"No, I didn't ask for a dollar. I asked do you know where you live?" Wolf huffed, he was beginning to get frustrated with the little girl, but at the end of the day he knew it wasn't the little girl's fault. "Where's your mother?"

"Candy." The little girl said with her hand still held out.

"No, I don't have no candy." Wolf huffed, the more he spoke to the little girl, the more he wanted to whip her parent's ass. Before Wolf could say another word to the little girl he heard a female voice coming from behind him.

"Mmm mmm mmm damn!"

Wolf turned and found a slim dark skin chick with a scarf on her head, house shoes on her feet and a pair of bright yellow booty shorts looking at his ass.

"Yo this your daughter?" Wolf asked trying to suppress his anger.

"I'm Yolanda." The dark skin chick extended her hand disregarding Wolf's original question as if it wasn't important.

"Wolf." He shook Yolanda's hand and when he tried to pull it back she was reluctant to let it go.

"You must be new around here." Yolanda licked her fully glossed lips seductively. "And I want to be the first to tell you it's a pleasure to meet you...and since I met you first I got first dibs."

"First dibs on what?" Wolf asked with a confused look on his face.

Yolanda's eyes immediately moved down to Wolf's crotch and a naughty smile flashed across her face.

"You really ain't from around here." The look on Yolanda's face told Wolf that in between her legs was getting wetter and wetter with each word she spoke.

"Listen Yolanda" Wolf said in a neutral tone."Your daughter was out in the middle of the street and I almost hit her by accident. You need to keep a better eye on her next time."

Yolanda's head snapped and shot daggers at the little girl. Before Wolf even knew what was going on, Yolanda ran over and started beating the little girl like she was an adult. "What the fuck I told....you...about playing....in that....god damn street!"

Wolf looked on in shock with a disgusted look on his face as he watched Yolanda beat the little girl because her parenting skills were horrible. Instead of teaching the child the danger of playing in the street, Yolanda decided to go upside the little girl's head instead. The way she was hitting the little girl Wolf could tell that this wasn't Yolanda first time committing an act like this, in public at that. The little girl screamed at the top of her lungs while Yolanda continued abusing the little girl.

Wolf looked around and noticed that other people paid the abuse no mind and walked past like this was normal or an everyday type of thing.

"Yo chill you wilding right now." Wolf stepped in, calling himself helping out. He grabbed Yolanda and pulled her off of the child. "That's enough; I think she learned her lesson."

Yolanda spun with the swiftness of a cat and swung on Wolf. "Don't put ya motherfucking hands on me....nigga is you crazy!"Wolf easily blocked Yolanda's punch. "Just get your daughter out of the street...please."

"Don't be telling me how to be a mother you punk ass bitch!" by now all of Yolanda's loud yelling had drawn a crowd.

Wolf knew that being in the wrong hood at the wrong time was how a lot of people got shot and he didn't want things to escalate any further. Before he got a chance to defuse the situation Ivy hopped out the car and turned the situation from bad to worse.

"Bitch, who the fuck you swinging on like you stupid?" Ivy barked. Witnessing another woman swing on her man didn't sit well with her nor was it something that she planned on ignoring or let slide.

Immediately Wolf grabbed Ivy and kept her and Yolanda separated. "Chill!" Wolf yelled in Ivy's face told her. "You pregnant remember?" He reminded her. While he kept Ivy restrained Yolanda crept around and tried to steal on Ivy. The punch landed and hit Ivy on the top of her head, Wolf swiftly spun around and pushed Yolanda back in an attempt to get her up off of Ivy, but apparently he didn't know his own strength because his push sent Yolanda stumbling backwards until she finally hit the ground. On her way down to the ground Yolanda stumbled over her daughter sending both of them crashing down to the ground in a dramatic fashion that made it look worse than it really was.

Wolf went to go and try to help Yolanda and her daughter up off the ground, he extended a helpful hand trying to get a handle on the situation, but in the hood things didn't work out so smoothly and as usual things went from one to ten in a split second.

"What the fuck is you doing cuz!?" Wolf looked up and saw a big black greasy looking motherfucker pushing through the crowd. The big man wore a dingy wife beater, tan khaki shorts, socks pulled all the way up to his knees and a pair of white *Chuck Taylors* with blue laces. Wolf also noticed a blue bandana hanging out of the man's left back pocket.

"Yo fam." Wolf began in a calm tone. "Listen I saw this little girl in the middle of the street and I was just trying to help her so..."

"Maniac I saw this fool trying to kidnap our daughter." Yolanda lied. "Then when I tried to stop him he jawed me." Her voice was loud and attracted the attention of the entire community.

"Go get back in the car." Wolf whispered in Ivy's ear. He could already see that this situation wasn't going to end smoothly. Unfortunately ignorance only respected violence, it was sad, but the truth. Wolf's main concern was making sure that Ivy was safe especially since she was now carrying his child in her stomach.

"I don't want to leave you." Ivy said softly. It was reasons like this she didn't want him trying to help everyone. Some people just had to be left behind point, blank, period and this was one of those situations. Ivy didn't want to leave Wolf, but at the same time she didn't want to look defiant out in public, so she did as Wolf told her and went and got back in the car.

"What's cracking!" Maniac threw his hands up and took an aggressive step forward.

Wolf moved like a blur, closing the distance between him and Maniac in less than a second. Maniac had his guards up, but Wolf's hands were quick. Before Maniac even knew he was in a fight, Wolf had already bashed him in the jaw twice. Not giving the big man a chance to regroup or gain any momentum Wolf fired off a vicious, painful looking combination, followed by a kick in between Maniac's legs causing him to crumble down to his knees.

"Man is you crazy? Talking like you built." Wolf growled as he continued to unload on the big man. "I'm tryna help get ya stupid ass daughter out of the street!"

While Wolf was pounding the big man out, another kid crept up on him from behind and sucker punched him in the back of the head. Once Yolanda saw the next man jump in the fight she quickly followed suit. She jumped on Wolf's back screaming a bunch of curse words as she attempted to choke him out. By now Maniac had made it back up to his feet and turned the fight into a three on one.

Not being the one to sit back and watch her man take a beating, Ivy threw the car in reverse and backed up all the way until she reached her and Wolf's apartment. Ivy sprung from the front seat and ran inside the apartment like a track star. Her man was in trouble so she had to move quick. Ivy ran to the closet in her bedroom and removed Wolf's 9mm from the shoe box. She quickly ran back outside with the gun in her hand, hopped back inside her car and headed back towards the rumble.

By the time Ivy made it back to the rumble she saw the big greasy looking nigga with a garage can held high above his head, she watched as he violently tossed the garbage can down on who she assumed was Wolf. When the garbage can made contact with its target the crowd erupted in a loud "ooooooooooooooooooh!!!"

Ivy quickly jumped out the car, raised the gun in the air and fired off three loud thunderous shots that sent the crowd scattering and car alarms wailing. She had no intention of shooting anyone, unless she *had* too. Once the crowd cleared Ivy spotted Wolf struggling back to his feet. His face was covered in blood, shirt ripped into shreds and he had an out of this world headache.

"You alright?" Ivy asked draping Wolf's arm across her neck as she helped him back to the car. By now she would or expected the police to arrive, but there was no sign of a cop car or police officer in sight.

"I'm good." Wolf lied. He was dizzy and felt like he had a concussion, but there was no way that he'd admit that to Ivy. In her eyes he was super man and today was no acceptation. Wolf took the gun from Ivy's hand before sliding in the passenger seat of the car. A simple task of going to the supermarket had turned into Wolf almost getting himself killed and from the looks on the faces of the people in the community Wolf could tell that the beef was far from over.

Chapter Eight

MURDER

Dice pulled the trigger and painted the wall with a petty drug dealers brains. Dice, The Big Show and a few other Spade members stood inside a local stash house that belonged to Prince. Amongst them lay several dead hustlers. Dice decided it was time to start fighting fire with fire. The Spades were no longer out to clean up the streets, they were now at war, an unnecessary war, but war was still war.

Dice knew that if Wolf was around, he would have been highly disappointed in him and what The Spades had become. The same streets that Wolf had risked his life for was no longer a safe environment for children to play, Dice, Psycho and Prince had turned the streets that Wolf had tried so hard to clean into a war zone. Each and every night more and more innocent bystanders were turning up dead. Innocent hard working civilians dead. Dice felt responsible for what was going on in the streets. He was doing the best he could, but his best wasn't seeming like enough these days. The Spades couldn't clean up the streets while going to war.

"Any word on Psycho's where abouts?" Dice asked. All of the killing was beginning to frustrate him and he was ready to get this over and done with.

"That clown Snow supposed to be performing at some rowdy ass club downtown tonight." The Big Show announced. "It's possible the Prince and Psycho might show their face in the club tonight."

Dice looked down at his watch, pulled out his cell phone and dialed Tonya's number. He just wanted to notify her that he'd be in a little late tonight. Dice frowned after the phone rang a few times, then the voicemail picked up. *"Where the fuck is she at?"* He wondered. After work Tonya always went to pick up their son and went straight home, so for her not to be answering the phone was strange. But at the moment Dice had more important things to worry about.

"So we gon hit this club or what?" The Big Show asked. "I think there's a good chance that we'll run into them fools in there."

"Let's do it." Dice replied. He was now the leader of The Spades and it was time to start leading by example and let all the other members see why Wolf had left him in charge of running the organization.

***

The roped off V.I.P. section in the club was off the chain. Ballers, goons, gold diggers, strippers and prostitutes flooded the section. Sexual predators disguised as perfect gentleman and gold diggers disguised as respectable ladies floated around the club in search of a victim, but the majority of the females in the club were there to see Snow.

Snow, Prince, Psycho and a few other men stood around laughing and joking while getting their drink on. "I should knock you the fuck out right now." Prince said looking at Bobby Dread with a disrespectful look on his face. "What's up with you?" He said finally cracking a smile. "I see you still wearing that dumb ass trench coat." Prince said causing everyone to erupt with laughter.

Bobby Dread shook his head and gave Prince a sad look. "You a funny nigga."

"Leave that nigga alone." Psycho said laughing hysterically.

"Nah, fuck that!" Prince continued. "I'm tired of this nigga wearing that dirty ass coat. Shit look filthy."

The more everyone laughed, the more upset Bobby Dread was becoming. The look on his face was a look of anger mixed with a sprinkle of embarrassment.

"This nigga scaring all the bitches away." Prince took a swig from his bottle, laughed and continued, "When the last time you got some pussy?"

Bobby Dread turned and shot daggers at Prince with his eyes, but still remained silent.

"And I ain't talking about no fat bitches either, When the last time you got some *real* pussy?" Prince laughed and draped his arm around Psycho's shoulder. "Nigga ain't had pussy since pussy had him..."

"Quit while you're ahead." Bobby Dread growled. "I'm warning you."

"No, I'm warning you to stop wearing that dirty ass trench coat." Prince continued. He was drunk and just fucking with Bobby Dread like he always did about his trench coat.

"Leave that nigga alone." Psycho said pulling the attention away from Bobby Dread before emotions and pride got in the way and caused a misunderstanding.

"I'm tired of looking at that bum ass coat that nigga need to burn that shit." Prince took another swig from his bottle. "You ain't in Jamaica no more motherfucker!" He yelled over at Bobby Dread. "Nigga been in America for mad long now still wearing a motherfucking trench coat...that's crazy...you know what?" He tilted the bottle up to his lips, "I'm bout to go fuck with one of these ratchet hoes that's what I'm bout to do."

Psycho shook his head as he watched Prince wander off into the crowd with Tall Man close on his heels. Psycho made a mental note to keep an eye on Prince with him being drunk and all.

Psycho raised his bottle up to his lips when he saw Monica arguing with a bouncer at the entrance of the V.I.P. section. *"Fuck is she doing here?"* He said to himself as he walked over there to see what was going on.

"Listen," The big bald bouncer's voice boomed, "You ain't getting up in here, now beat it." he said dismissively.

"Now beat it?"Monica echoed. Looking at the bouncer like he was crazy. "Nigga you must be drunk right now....when *my man* finds out how greasy you over here talking he gon clap fire out ya stupid ass."

"Word?" The bounder said.

"Word to my mother, you watch and see." Monica said fire dancing in her eyes. If she had a gun right now she would of shot the bouncer dead for trying to style on her like her man's name didn't ring bells.

"Not for nothing." The bouncer said. "But who's your man? Just curious."

"Psycho." Monica announced proudly.

The bouncer broke out into a laughing fit. Looking from a distance one would of thought that Monica had just told the bouncer a hilarious joke. The bouncer was laughing so hard that his eyes began to water. "Oh shit girl. You a funny motherfucker." The bouncer continued to laugh right in Monica's face as if she was invisible. "Better not let Psycho's *real* girlfriend hear you say some dumb sit like that."

Monica was so hurt by the bouncer's words. The truth cut through her like a knife. Not having a good come back line, Monica decided that she would just spit in the bouncer's face and call it even. Before Monica got a chance to commit the disgusting act, Psycho showed up right on time.

"Yo Mike, she's cool let her in." Psycho called out to the bouncer.

"I'mma let her in, but keep her away from the drinks cause she talking *crazy* talking about she's *your* girl." The bouncer said with a questioning eye brow.

"Nah, this my cousin." Psycho said saying the first thing that came to his mind. "She probably figured if she ain't name drop that you wouldn't let her in, but yo, I'mma holla at you later." Psycho said as him and Monica disappeared into the V.I.P. section.

Psycho led Monica over to a secluded section, then turned and faced her. "Fuck is you doing here?"

"Oh, so I'm your cousin now?" Monica said with a nasty look on her face. "Word Psycho, that's how you tryna play it?"

"Monica you already know..."

"You already know my ass!" Monica barked cutting Psycho off. "Tell that shit to one of them *other* stupid bitches. What you ashamed of me or something? If you don't wanna fuck with a bitch no more all you gotta do is say so, cause all that cousin shit ain't gon work!"

Psycho tilted his bottle up to his lips and took a quick sip. The look on his face said that he could care less what Monica was rambling about. "You finish?"

"Fuck you mean am I finished?" Monica's face c rumbled up, "You playing yourself right now, but it's cool cause the dick ain't all that anyway." She yelled trying to make it known that her and Psycho had been intimate with one another.

"Listen you stupid motherfucker!" Psycho growled, "I told you a hundred times that if we deal, then it would have to be on the low cause I have a girl and trust me you don't want..."

"Fuck Pauleena!" Monica shouted causing a few heads to turn in their direction following the outburst.

"Bitch!" Psycho's hand shot out and wrapped around Monica's throat, "I didn't I tell you about ya stupid ass mouth." He barked as he raised his bottle and began splashing champagne in Monica's weave, then gave her a stiff shove. Monica almost broke her ankle in the tall heels she was wearing as she fell back into a small coffee table that decorated the V.I.P. section knocking down a row of bottles on her way down to the floor. The loud commotion caused the same big bald headed bouncer to run over to the scene. He roughly yanked Monica up to her feet and escorted her out the V.I.P. kicking and screaming.

"Stupid ass bitch." Psycho mumbled as he picked up another bottle and popped it open. As he got ready to take a sip he noticed a medium built African nigga in a tight muscle shirt grilling him. "Problem?"

The African man stood to his feet. "You dead wrong for doing that black queen like that homie."

"You joking right?" Psycho turned the bottle in his hand up and took a sip.

"I don't joke when it comes to my queens." The African said in a serious tone. "You young *boys* don't have no respect nowadays, what kind of fool disrespects their *own people*?"

"You know shorty from somewhere or something?" Psycho asked.

"I don't have to know her, that queen you just disrespected could of been someone's wife or maybe even someone's sister." The African pointed out.

"Was she *your* wife or *your* sister?" Psycho asked.

"That's not the point..."

"Then shut the fuck up!" Psycho spat.

"Listen brother, I'm the last person you want to disrespect." The African man said taking as aggressive step towards Psycho. "I'm not a defenseless woman, you not gon just shove me down to the floor and that be the end of the story, in my country we kill tigers with our bare hands, then afterwards...."

Psycho violently busted the African man over top of his head with the bottle he was holding in his hand. He made sure he turned his head as glass sprayed all over the place making sure to not let any glass get in his eyes.

The African man stumbled back into the rail with a dazed look in his eyes. Psycho could tell that the man was out cold on his feet. Psycho slapped him viciously across the mouth, drawing blood, he followed up with a nasty hook to the jaw as he watched the African man flip over the rail like a wrestler being closed lined over the top rope. Everybody in the V.I.P looked on in shock as they watched Psycho snuff the African man and witnessed his body flip over the rail and fall all the way to the lower level of the club down to the dance floor.

Psycho leaned over the rail looked down and saw the African sprawled out on the floor with a crowd around him "Stupid ass African nigga."

"You alright?" Bobby Dread asked.

"Yeah, I'm good."

"You hit that didn't you?" Bobby Dread asked.

"Huh?" The question had caught Psycho off guard.

"Shorty that just got escorted out of here, you hit that didn't you?" Bobby Dread asked with a devilish smile. "Don't worry your secret is safe with me." He said, then spun off leaving Psycho alone in h is thoughts.

***

Snow sat in a comfortable looking couch on the other side of the V.I.P. section with a drink in his hand. A bad bitch that he had just met by his side and a bunch of goons lurked throughout the section. They were supposed to be looking for any signs of trouble, but instead they were the ones who were looking to start some trouble. As Snow sat bobbing his head to the music that bumped through the speakers he noticed a chick in a pink dress who's face looked familiar, but he couldn't place where he had knew shorty from. "*I know that bitch from somewhere."* Snow said to himself. Just as he got up to approach the woman a loud commotion broke out at the entrance. Several white men entered the club with bright lights on top of their cameras. The Terminator smoothly walked inside the club flanked by his three hundred pound personal security guard that went by the name Bear. Women screamed and threw themselves at The Terminator only to have Bear violently push and shove his adoring public away. The camera crew fought and struggled to catch the Terminator's every move on film.

The Terminator was officially a star and the face of boxing. He had made appearances in several of the hottest rappers music videos including one of Snow's videos. All of the hype was about The Terminator agreeing to fight a man with a perfect record consisting of "35-0" with 34 knockouts, the word in the boxing world was that "Brutus the Russian Sensation" was the hardest hitting man in the business, there was also a nasty rumor that the Russian boxer was on steroids and had super natural strength. The Terminator vs. Brutus the Russian Sensation was the fight that the world wanted to see and The Terminator planned on giving the fans what they wanted to see.

"What's good my nigga?" The Terminator gave Snow dap.

"Yo what's up? I heard the big announcement today." Snow smiled. "You signed on to fight Brutus the Russian sensation in his backyard that's some gutsy shit."

The Terminator shrugged. "This what I do." He said cockily. All the jewelry he wore had to add up to around a million dollars. In his mind he was a star and stars were supposed to shine.

"What's all the camera's for?" Snow asked.

"Promotion for the big fight." The Terminator smiled as a light skin woman almost broke her neck just to touch him.

As Snow sat talking to The Terminator it clicked in his mind where he recognized the woman in the pink dress from. She was with Live Wire that night at the restaurant when Live Wire had stole on him.

Snow walked over and roughly grabbed the woman. In a quick motion he raised his hand to strike the woman, but The Terminator caught his hand before he could deliver the blow.

"You wilding right now." The Terminator whispered in Snow's ear and nodded towards his camera crew that was filming everything. "Save it for another time."

"You right, you right." Snow nodded. "Let me go get ready to hit the stage." He gave The Terminator a pound, then spun off.

The Terminator turned and faced the beautiful woman in the pink dress, "Sorry about that, my friend had a little too much to drink. The Terminator." He extended his hand.

"Lisa." She replied squinting form the bright lights that rested on top of the camera the white man held aimed directly at them.

"Come have a drink with me." The Terminator said leading Lisa over to an empty table.

***

Down on the dance floor Prince and Tall Man stood over in the cut against the wall, sipping from his bottle and watching the scantily clad young ladies pass. A woman wearing a white half see through tube skirt caught Prince's eye. "Shorty right there got that cake." He nodded towards the chick in the white dress ass.

Tall Man glanced at the woman's ass and nodded his head. Silently agreeing with Prince. "Bet you can't get that." He challenged.

Prince looked at Tall Man like he had lost his mind. "You speaking to the Prince right now. You know that right?" He said like that was supposed to mean something. Prince watched as the chick in the white dress ass shook like it had a mind of its own. From the way the woman danced Prince could tell that she was looking for attention from a nigga that had his bread right. "$5,000 I bag shorty."

"Bet." Tall Man said as him and Prince bumped fists.

Prince took a swig from his bottle and headed towards the woman in the white dress on his way over towards the chick he accidentally stepped on a man's fresh white air force one's.

"Fuck is you blind motherfucker!" The man's who foot had been stepped on barked as he pushed Prince up off of him. He then glanced down at the dirt mark on his brand new white sneakers, the dirt mark only passed him off even further.

"My bad." Prince said humbly. He was having a good night and didn't want to ruin it by having to send someone to the hospital over some foolishness.

"My bad my motherfucking ass!" The man barked as two of his homeboys came and flanked him. "Nigga you better cough up some bread so I can get me a new pair of kicks!" He said in an overly aggressive tone as if any second he was about to go upside Prince's head.

While the man who's shoes had been stepped on continued his rant, he didn't even notice Tall Man slip behind him and his two cronies.

"Listen fam," Prince slurred with a smirk on his face. "Knock the tough Toney act off before you get yourself hurt. I don't give a fuck about you or them raggedy ass sneakers."

"I hear that fly shit." The man shot back, then in a quick motion he tossed a drink in Prince's face. "How bout that?"

Prince quickly removed his .40 cal from his waistband at the sight of the gun the man who had tossed the drink in Prince's face almost shitted on himself. Prince swung the gun with all his might and hit the man across his face with the gun knocking him out cold. "You stupid motherfucker you wanna die over some stupid ass sneakers...huh...I see...you ain't talking shit....now!" Prince huffed as he continued to pistol whip the clown that laid unconscious. The man's two homeboys acted as if they were about to try and break up the fight, when Tall man stabbed one of the men in their back, then cut the other one across the face, sending them running as far away from the knife in the Tall Man's hand as possible.

"That's enough." Tall Man huffed as he struggled to get Prince up off the unconscious man that laid before them. Prince gave the man one last kick to the ribs.

"I'm good." Prince said brushing imaginary dirt from his shirt. "Come with me to the bathroom real quick." Prince stuck his .40 cal back in his waist band as him and Tall Man headed in the direction of the bathrooms.

Chapter Nine

A Bloody Mess

The Gambino Brother's stood up against the wall in the cut watching Psycho and his crew ball out. They watched as Psycho and his team purchased $300 dollar bottles of champagne by the case just to pour it in the mouths of women who were into that type of thing. Bottles of champagne were being passed around like they were bottles of water and the sight alone disgusted them.

"That's just why the black race is fucked up now." Victor hissed. He didn't call himself a racist; he just couldn't stand anybody of a different race or color. "Motherfuckers get a little bit of money and lose they fucking minds." he shook his head sadly.

As the Gambino Brother's continued to keep a close eye on Psycho and his crew, they noticed one of Psycho's boys get into a little altercation on the dance floor that left one man's face bashed in and two of his friends on the business end of a sharp blade. A smile appeared on Alex Gambino's face when he saw two of Psycho's boys heading towards the bathroom.

"Go take care of that and I'll back you up." Alex Gambino said. He wasn't able to get his shot gun inside the club tonight so he had to settle for a 9mm with an extended clip that held 32 shots.

"Bout fucking time." Victor Gambino huffed, then took off in the direction of the bathroom. Once Alex saw his brother enter the bathroom, he quickly walked over towards the bathroom and guarded the door making sure no one went in and the only one that would be coming out alive was his bother.

***

By the time Dice and The Spades arrived at the club, the line had already began to snake up the block. Teenage boys and girls hustled up and down the street's wearing Snow and M.O.E. paraphernalia promoting his performance and brand like he was Jay-Z or somebody. The sidewalk was crowded with mostly half naked women buzzing about the highly anticipated performance by Snow.

Dice, The Big Show and around ten Spades members walked towards the entrance wearing all black. When they reached the front door they were met by a big heavy set mean looking bouncer.

"Fuck y'all niggaz thin y'all going?" The bouncer asked in a deep voice, flexing his muscles like he was a wrestler.

"We got some important business to take care of in this club tonight." Dice spoke in a calm tone. "If you don't mind letting us inside so we can resolve this matter as quick as possible and be out of your way."

"Fuck y'all supposed to be the new Wu-Tang clan?" The bouncer said laughing hysterically at his own joke. "Take that shit to the back of the line before I get upset."

"What!?" Dice barked, his entire body language was hostile, changing the whole vibe of the conversation.

The Big Show quickly stepped in before the situation went spiraling out of control. "Listen Big Man." he said pulling out a wad of cash, "Here" he said pulling two bills out of the wad and handed it to the bouncer.

The bouncer eyed the two twenties like they had been rinsed in throw up. "What I'm supposed to do with this go buy me a happy meal?"

"What's your price?" The Big Show asked trying to hide his frustration.

"Three large." The bouncer smiled knowing whatever price he set the men were going to pay it especially since everyone wanted to see Snow's performance tonight.

"This shit don't make no motherfucking sense." The Big Show huffed as he slapped three hundred dollar bills in the bouncer's chunky hand.

"It was nice doing business with you gentlemen...thanks." The bouncer said, then moved to the side so the men dressed in all black could enter the club.

"Thanks my ass!" The Big Show huffed. "Nigga you better give me my forty dollars back."

"Oh." The bouncer said as if he had forgotten that quick. He slapped the two twenties in The Big Show's hand, then watched as the men in all black entered the club.

Dice stepped foot in the club with a mean look on his face. The whole altercation at the front door had him pissed off; he wanted so badly to clap the bouncer at the front door. French Montana's remix to the reggae classic *"Freak"* banged through the speakers and had the club rocking. Instantly through all the party animals Dice spotted Psycho over in the V.I.P. with The Terminator in the upper level sipping champagne and tossing money up in the air as if it had been grown on trees.

Witnessing the ignorant act only pissed Dice off even further. He glanced over at The Big Show, then nodded in Psycho's direction. The Big Show replied with a simple head nod. Dice bumped his way through the crowd, side stepping couples getting their freak on and men standing around fronting like they were the toughest thing since "Mr.T".

As Dice snaked his way through the crowd, a couple blocked his path. A diesel looking man with dread locks stood shirtless as sweat covered his entire body, his hips swayed and gyrated to the reggae beat that bumped through the speakers. In front of him a woman in a half see through white dress stood bent over touching the floor grinding her big jiggly ass all up on the man with the dreads.

In a quick smooth motion the man with the dreads spun the woman in the white dress around and lifted her up in the air. He lifted her up above his head, the woman, then quickly wrapped her legs around the diesel man's neck, his head slipping right up under her dress. From the outside looking in it looked as if the man with the dreads was eating the woman in the white dress pussy in mid-air right there on the dance floor.

The woman in the white dress yelled, moaned and made faces like the man whose head was in between her legs was really eating her pussy and from the look on her face she was enjoying every second of it.

Dice went to side step the couple, but stopped dead in his tracks when he looked up at the woman who was in the air with her legs wrapped around the man with the dread's neck moaning like a phone sex operator.

He squinted his eyes to get a better look at the woman in the white see through dress. *"You gotta be shitting me."* He said out loud. The woman in the white see through dress was none other than Tonya. Dice didn't say a word instead he just stood back and continued to watch the show.

A few seconds passed before Tonya locked eyes with Dice and from the look on his face she knew she was in big trouble.

"Yo, put me down!" Tonya yelled to the man with the dreads as if him tossing her up in the air was a problem all of a sudden. She quickly pulled down her dress and walked over to Dice. "Hey baby wassup? What you doing here?" She asked opening her arms for a hug.

"I should be asking you that." Dice said declining her hug.

"Nothing just *dancing."* Tonya said as if being tossed in the air getting her pussy ate was the latest dance move.

"That's how niggaz *dance* now a days?" Dice asked with a raised brown. He was seconds away from smacking the shit out of Tonya and dragging her out of the club by her hair.

"What's the big deal?" Tonya spat. "You know niggaz be wilding in the club."

"No, it looked like you was the one *wilding*." Dice pointed out. "Where's my son?"

"With my mother."

"Why ain't he with his *own* mother?"

"Look!" Tonya said as if Dice was becoming an annoyance. "I'm tired of sitting in the house by myself; you ain't never home no more. A relationship consists of two people." She waved two fingers in Dice's face. "I can't be in a relationship when I'm alone *all the time*."

"Listen you stupid mother...."

"Is it necessary for you to talk to me like that?" Tonya sucked her teeth, "You know what, never mind, it don't even matter."

"Never mind what?" Dice pressed. Tonya was really embarrassing him in front of The Spades and he was seconds away from putting his foot up her ass.

"It doesn't even matter." Tonya huffed.

Tonya and Dice's conversation was interrupted when the Diesel man with the dreads walked up. "Everything alright over here?" He asked Tonya, but his eyes were locked on Dice.

"Yeah, I'm good, thanks Maurice." Tonya said smiling from ear to ear, like her and the man were childhood friends.

"Aight if you need me I'll be right over there." the man with the dreads kissed Tonya on the cheek, then looked Dice up and down before he blacked off.

Dice looked at Tonya and could see all 32 of her teeth. "So since I'm not *never* home you take it upon yourself to come to the club and let a nigga eat your pussy in front of everybody? That's what we doing now?"

"He wasn't eating my pussy." Tonya snapped, "I told you we were just dancing."

"Do you even got any panties on?" Dice went to reach up under Tonya's dress, but she quickly swatted his hand away and took a step back.

"Why you sweating me for?" Tonya fanned herself with her hand; the heat in the club was beginning to feel like a furnace. "If you so worried about me the way you *acting* like you are, then why do I have to fight for your time and attention?"

"Listen." Dice sighed loudly, "Go home. We'll finish this conversation at the house."

"No!" Tonya said defiantly. "I'll leave when you leave and we'll leave together."

"Listen some serious shit about to go down in here tonight and I don't need you getting caught up in this foolishness." Dice explained. "Now get up outta here and I'll see you back at the house."

"You must think I'm stupid." Tonya spat looking Dice up and down. "You want me to go home so you and your boys can have a good time with all these ratchet ass hoes up in here. Naw nigga I don't think so.We leaving this motherfucker together." The nerve of Tonya to call somebody else ratchet, wasn't nobody else in the club getting tossed up in the air getting their pussies eaten out, but her. All Dice could do was shake his head. When he got back home he planned on whipping Tonya's ass then kicking her out the whip (dump her).

Dice went to walk past Tonya when the loud sound of gun fire erupted throughout the club followed by the deafening sound of a machine gun fire. Instantly everyone ducked and dropped down to the floor, seconds later a full stampede broke out as club goers pushed, shoved and broke their necks trying to get out of the club without getting hit by a stray bullet.

***

“You should of let me kill that motherfucker.” Prince said out loud as he looked back at his reflection in the mirror. He couldn’t believe the nerve of the punk who called himself getting crazy with him over some sneakers.

“Not worth it.” Tall Man said, “Too many witnesses.”

Before Prince could reply he heard the bathroom door bust open and in walked a Spanish or Dominican looking man holding a .45 in each hand.

“Down on the floor now!” Victor Gambino barked. The tone of his voice was deadly, so was the look in his eyes.

Prince and Tall Man looked at each other, then looked back at the gun man like he spoke a foreign language, pride and ego’s stopped them from cooperating.

Boc!

Tall Man spilled down to the bathroom floor clutching his thigh rolling around in agony. He didn’t expect for the gun man to really shoot him, especially with them having so many goons roaming around the club.

Victor trained his .45’s on Prince. “You gon make me repeat myself?”

Prince glanced down at the dirty, wet, sticky floor, then back up at the gun man. “Fuck that, you gon have to shoot me.” He said ignorantly.

Boc!

“Arrgh!...shit!” Prince growled as he hit the floor hard clutching his thigh. He didn’t have a clue who the gun man was, but whoever he was he was now living on borrowed time.

Victor Gambino quickly removed Tall Man and Prince’s hammers from their waist, before stripping them of all their jewels and money.

“You know who I am?” Prince hissed with a murderous scowl on his face. “I’m the Prince.”

“Never heard of you, keep banging!” Victor Gambino brought the heel of his Gore Tex Boot down across Prince’s nose breaking it. Once he had what he had come for Victor exited the bathroom and spotted a man with long wild looking dread locks and an old looking trench coat aiming an assault rifle at his brother.

With the quickness of a snake Victor ran and tackled Alex down to floor. Just the sound of the assault rifle banged loudly.

***

Bobby Dread stood over in the cut hollering at a washed up looking white girl. Prince's words had really hurt him and had him feeling a certain type of way, so now to prove to everyone including himself that he could in fact get a woman and get some *real pussy* as Prince called it.

"So what you like to do for fun?" Bobby Dread asked. His game was super whack and he knew it, that was the reason he mainly dealt with prostitutes and fat bitches.

"Huh?" The white girl asked with a confused look on her face. She wasn't really for all the small talk. She wanted to get her brains fucked out, she needed to get her brains fucked out, she wanted to be fucked out by a black man. The word was once you go black, you never go back and she was curious to see if this myth was in fact true or not. "You sure do talk a lot." The white girl said seductively running her index finger up and down Bobby Dreads chest, while feeling him up. The white girl's hand rubbed against Bobby Dreads bullet proof vest. "Ooooh you one of those bad boys huh?" She grinned as if him being active in the streets made her pussy get wet. "Do you shoot a lot of people?" She asked in a drunken slur.

"I don't know what you talking about." Bobby Dread said quickly, not sure if the white girl was wearing a wire or not.

"Am I asking you too many question…huh?" The white girl said pressing her breast up against Bobby Dread's vest. "If you want me to be quiet, then why don't you put something in my mouth?" She slurred looking up into Bobby Dreads eyes, one hand held Bobby Dread's lower back, while her other hand found its way to his dick. She rubbed and massaged his dick through his jeans until she got the reaction she was looking for. "Oh my."She giggled with a shocked expression on her face.

"We do *big* things around here." Bobby Dread boasted.

"I see." The white girl licked her lips. "Can I taste it? Please can I taste it?" She begged, her eyes pleading.

"Yeah, I got you later."

"No!" The white girl snapped. "I wanna taste it now!" She said as she slowly melted down to her knees and began undoing Bobby Dread's pants. Once she got a hold of Bobby Dread's dick the white girl put it in her mouth and began sucking on it as if it were a pacifier.

Bobby Dread moved his hips up, went deeper inside the white woman's face and began to feed her dick. He played in the woman's hair, talked dirty to her and watched her gag every now and again.

"Check ya man out though." The Terminator laughed draping his arm around Psycho's neck and pointed over in Bobby Dread's direction.

Psycho peered over at Bobby Dread and all he could do was shake his head. He was glad to finally see Bobby Dread having a good time and enjoying himself. The sight alone put a smile on Psycho's face.

Bobby Dread had his way with the white woman's mouth until he stiffened up, grabbed a handful of the white girl's blond hair, released a loud grunt and shot his loud.

The white girl swallowed and wiped her mouth with the back of her hand, then flashed a devilish smile. "Delicious."

Before Bobby Dread got a chance to reply, he noticed a minor scuffle breakout on the dance floor that involved Prince and Tall Man, once he was sure that Prince had control of the situation, he was getting ready to take his new white friend in the back and bust her ass until he noticed a half Spanish, half Mexican looking cat following closely behind Prince. The Mexican man didn't have stick up kid written all over him, but he definitely screamed trouble. Next Bobby Dread noticed another Mexican looking cat head over to the bathroom door and post up out front, every two seconds his eyes scanned from left to right.

Bobby Dread tried calling over to Psycho to get his attention, but him and The Terminator were being entertained by a few half naked divas over in the cut, plus with the music being so loud made it damn near impossible for Psycho to hear anything.

*"Fuck it."*Bobby Dread said to himself as he headed for the bathroom. He opened up his trench coat and held his the A.K. behind his leg as he pushed and shoved his way through the sea of people who stood between him and the bathroom. The closer he made it to the bathroom the more he could tell that the man who stood out front guarding the bathroom was indeed going to be a problem, but luckily for him Bobby Dread kept his problem solver with him at *all* times.

***

Alex Gambino stood out front the bathroom, scanning his surroundings. Unlike his bother Victor, Alex wasn't racist and his sexual preferences were black women, but he had to admit *these* black people were unlike any he had ever seen. Alex Gambino loved black women, but had never been to a club with this many *drunk* black people in his life. He was learning firsthand the difference between niggaz and drunk niggaz. Alex bobbed his head to the beat trying to fit in with the rest of the crowd that was until he noticed a kid with a mouth full of gold teeth swaying from side to side headed in his direction.

"Whoa, whoa!" Alex Gambino said placing a firm hand on the black kid's chest that was covered with several fake gold chains. "The bathroom is closed."

The kid with the gold teeth swiftly swatted Alex's hand from his chest. "Listen motherfucker!" The kid said in an aggressive tone, "Fuck is you the bathroom patrol? Nigga I need to get in there it's an emergency."

"What's the emergency?" Alex prodded.

"Nigga I gotta take a number seven now move!" The kid huffed, then tried to slip past Alex and ease his way inside the door that had the word "Men" written across the top in gold letters.

In a swift motion Alex throw a powerful elbow strike that landed square on the kid with the gold teeth's temple. The kid was out on his feet, but instead of him falling straight to the floor he stumbled back a few steps then crashed into a group of ladies then hit the floor.

"Damn my nigga!" Alex heard a female voice shout. He looked up and saw a voluptuous black woman staring at him with a hard mean look plastered on her face with a few of her home girls flanked behind her.

"You just pushed that nigga into me and made me spill my drink on this brand new Gucci dress I'm wearing!" The woman fussed as if it was a matter of life and death.

"I'm sorry." Alex said humbly. It was an honest mistake; he had no intentions on ruining the woman's Gucci dress that which upon further review Alex realized was a knock off.

"Sorry!" The voluptuous woman repeated. Instantly Alex could tell that the woman that stood before him had a little too much to drink. "Um Mister you *better* break me off with some bread for a new dress or cover the charge of my cleaners bill. I don't care which one, oh but you gonna give me something."

"Sorry, but unfortunately I don't have any cash on me right now." Alex said trying to prevent the situation from getting worse, but it seemed like the calmer he was, the more aggressive the voluptuous woman was becoming.

"Yo, my man that's word to my kids you gon give me something!" The chick barked, then went to tap Alex's pockets, Alex was on point and quickly blocked the woman's attempt.

"Yo chill."

"Fuck you mean chill!?" The chick raved then tossed her drink in Alex's face.

Splash!

Alex slowly wiped his face as he heard two gun shots echo from the other side of the bathroom door. He badly wanted to rip the woman's head off that stood in front of him, but he knew better, he knew what was at stake, knew nothing good would come from assaulting the drunk woman. So instead of stooping down to the drunk chick's level he decided to pretend that the drink incident never happened, that was until he looked up and saw the drunk chick with her hands up like she wanted to go toe to toe with him.

"That's right fuck his ass up KiKi!" He heard one of her home girls shout amping up the situation, turning the matter from bad to worse in a matter of seconds.

Alex didn't want to harm the woman that stood before him, from experience he could tell the woman was just trying to put on a show for her home girls, but what she didn't know was the man standing before her was as ruthless and vicious as they came and at any moment her life could be taking just like that.

Before the situation got further out of hand Alex Gambino noticed a big rough looking bouncer heading over in the direction at a quick pace.

"What's the problem over here!?" The bouncer's voice boomed as he towered over Alex.

"This wet back motherfucker here." The voluptuous chick pointed at Alex. "Pushed this other nigga into me and made me spill a drink on my new dress."

"Alright buddy let's go!" The bouncer barked roughly grabbing Alex by the collar of his shirt not even bothering to hear his side of the story.

Alex quickly removed his 9mm from his waistband and fired a shot into the bouncer's shin.

Boc!

Instantly the bouncer crumbled down to the sticky club floor clutching his leg, the look of shock, fear and pain resting in his eyes.

The gun shot had caused a minor stamped to take place, but through all the commotion Alex looked up and saw a man with dread locks aiming an A.K. 47 assault rifle in his direction.

Looking down the barrel of the big gun left Alex stuck, like a deer caught in the headlights. His heart dropped down into the pit of his stomach as death stared him in the face. Just as the man with the dreads squeezed down on the trigger, Alex felt a force from behind tackle him down to the floor as the sound of the assault rifle being fired filled the air.

Victor Gambino reached up from the floor and fired three rounds into Bobby Dread's direction.

Boc! Boc! Boc!

Bobby Dread managed to dodge one of the bullets, but the other hit him flush in his arm, the impact forcing him to take a few steps back.

"Come on we out!" Victor yelled as he helped Alex up to his feet, the two fired recklessly over their shoulders as they scrambled towards the exit along with the rest of the crowd.

Bobby Dread raised the A.K. with one hand and squeezed down on the trigger, he wasn't able to get off a good shot as the A.K. was way too powerful for him to control with one hand. He watched as bullets sprayed and hit everyone *except* for his intended target.

***

Psycho sat on the couch over in the cut sipping on a bottle of water. All the champagne and alcohol he consumed had his head spinning and feeling like he was in a whole other world. As psycho sat on the couch his thoughts were interrupted when he heard the sound of a woman's heels come to a stop directly in front of him. Psycho looked up and saw Monica standing there with as sad puppy look on her face. Her hair was pulled back into a loose raggedy looking ponytail. The dried up champagne caused her weave to look real hard and crusty like she may of applied *too much* spritz to her hair.

The corner of her eyes welled up and tears threatened to spill at any given second.

"You still here?" Psycho asked drily.

"Can we talk please?" Monica murmured. She could tell that Psycho was still upset and didn't want to upset him any further.

"Monica." Psycho released a dramatic sigh and massaged his temples. "We don't have nothing left to talk about, go on and enjoy your life I'm no good for you. All I'm going to wind up doing is getting you killed."

"Well I might as well die." Monica stated plainly, "Cause a life without you, ain't a life worth living."

"Knock it the fuck off with that dumb shit." Psycho spat. Monica was full of shit and he knew it. No matter how many times she apologized or said sorry, she always some how resorted back to doing the same dumb shit over and over again and quite frankly Psycho was sick of Monica and her foolish ways. "You just can't get right."

"I promise you that I can *get right*." Monica sang. "Please Psycho all I'm asking for is one last chance to prove myself to you. Please Daddy?"

"It's quiet." Psycho said in a dismissive manner.

"Please Psycho." Monica continued to beg. "*We* need each other."

Instantly Psycho's face crumbled up. "Fuck you mean *we*?" What you speak French now? Fuck is with all this *we* shit, it ain't no we and it ain't never gon be no we cause you don't know how to act."

"I promise if you give me this one last chance I'll get my act together." Monica begged, then melted down to her knees with her hands in a praying position. "Pleeeeeeeease Daddy….pleeeeease?"

"Get up!" Psycho spat quickly yanking Monica up off the floor as he looked over his shoulder making sure no one was witnessing the fool Monica was making of herself. "That's the shit I be talking about, why the fuck would you get down on your knees in front of all these people?"

"Fuck these people!" Monica spat. "You think I give a fuck about what these people think about me? All I care about is what you think about me, I'm sorry Psycho please don't be upset with me."

Before Psycho could respond the sound of machine gun fire filled the air. Instantly he knew the gun shots had to be coming from no other than Bobby Dread. It was only one person he knew who kept an assault rifle on him at all times.

Psycho pulled his P89 Rugar from its holster, his ears leading his eyes towards the action. He looked and saw two Mexican looking men firing recklessly over their shoulders. He then looked over at Bobby Dread and noticed that he was still on his feet, but slightly hunched over. Immediately he knew Bobby Dread had been hit, where at and how bad was the question. Before Psycho could rush over and check up on his comrade, he noticed quick movement out of the corner of his eye. He looked over and saw Dice along with several other Spades coming straight for him.

"Fuck!" Psycho cursed loudly. He quickly fired five shots over in The Spades direction not caring who or how many he hit. Once Psycho opened fire the rest of his crew quickly followed suite and turned the club into a battle field.

Psycho hopped over the couch and made a dash for the back exit, he was too drunk to be sitting trying to figure out what was what, or who was who. Psycho spilled out the back door of the club and quickly hopped behind the wheel of his silver B.M.W. before he got a chance to pull out of the parking spot he heard someone banging loudly on his passenger side window, out of reflex he quickly aimed his P89 at the sound, but didn't pull the trigger when he realized that it was Monica. Psycho quickly hit the unlock button and watched as Monica slid own into the passenger seat. Once Monica's door was closed Psycho stepped on the gas.

Scurrrr!

"Dam you was just about to leave a bitch for dead back there?" Monica huffed.

"Nah, I thought you was right behind me." Psycho lied. His eyes darted from the road, back up to the rearview mirror every five seconds.

"You aight?"

"I love you Psycho." Monica said ignoring Psycho's question.

"Not now Monica." Psycho brushed her off, he wasn't in the mod for Monica and her bullshit. Thoughts of dropping her off at the next corner and making her catch a cab crossed his mind several times, but for some reason Psycho just couldn't get rid of her.

"Can you please forgive me Daddy?" Monica whined.

"For what? So the next day you can go and do that same dumb shit?" Psycho huffed, his eyes glued to the rearview mirror. As Psycho was driving he felt Monica tugging at his zipper. "Yo, what you doing?"

Monica ignored Psycho and continued to work on his jeans until she had his dick sitting in the palm of her hands. Before Psycho could say another word, Monica spit on his dick then began jerking it at a fast pace. All while jerking Psycho's dick Monica continued spitting on it. "I'm sorry Daddy; can you please forgive me....pleeeeeeaasae?" She moaned.

A minute passed before Psycho could no longer take the torture any longer. He roughly gripped the back on Monica's head and forced her head down into his lap. Monica gripped the base of Psycho's dick firmly with one hand and cuffed his balls with the other hand. Her head bobbed up and down vigorously, while still jerking his dick at the same time. Animalistic sounds escaped from Monica's mouth as well as loud wet sucking noises.

"That's right get crazy on this dick." Psycho moaned. He could feel saliva dripping from his balls down to his ass crack. He forced Monica's head all the way down in his lap and held it there. Enjoying the sound of her gagging and choking on his length. “I want you to suck the sin off this dick.”

Psycho did his best to keep his eyes on the road as Monica swirled her head from side to side, she licked, kissed, sucked and slurped all over Psycho’s dick until she finally got it to erupt. Monica greedily swallowed every last drop and was still in search for more.

“Chill, that’s enough, you gon fuck around and make me crash.” Psycho said, trying to remove Monica’s head from his lap.

“Noooo.” Monica moaned. “I’m not finish with *him* yet.”

Psycho stopped at a red light. Trey Songz song, “Don’t you be scared.” Hummed softly through the speakers while Monica’s head remained down in his lap. Before the light turned green the sound of Psycho’s cell phone ringing could be heard. He glanced down and saw the number to the federal prison that Pauleena was being housed at flashing across the screen.

“Yo!” Psycho yelled, “This is Pauleena on the phone, I better not hear a peep out of you!” He warned her in a stern tone.

“Daddyyyyy, I told you I was going to be a good girl from now on.” Monica moaned, then buried her head back down in Psycho’s lap while he drove.

“Yo what’s up baby?” Psycho answered. He was nervous and scared that Monica might slip up and make a sudden strange noise and get him in a shit load of trouble, but he hadn’t spoken to Pauleena in a few days and was missing her like crazy and desperately wanted to hear her voice. “Where the fuck you been? You got me out here worried sick about you.”

“Sorry baby. I had to put a couple of these Spades bitches in they place.” Pauleena said. “You know regular jail shit.”

“You better be staying out of trouble while you in there.” Psycho lightly scolded here. “Nine more months and you’ll be home. Don’t fuck that up.”

"What you been up to lately?"

"Thinking about you and how tight that pussy gon be when you get out."

"You so nasty." Pauleena laughed. The truth was she too had been thinking about sex like crazy lately. Being away from a man for so long was starting to take its toll on Pauleena; she missed Psycho so much that the sound of his voice alone caused her to get wet. "When you gon come back up here again, so you can play with this pussy?"

"You know I'm up there every weekend." Psycho replied. Every week he made sure he made the four hour drive to go and visit his fiancé, he didn't believe in leaving his loved ones for dead when hard times came about.

"Any word on that clown Live Wire?" Pauleena asked, she hadn't forgotten about what Live Wire had done to her mother. Ms. Diaz was a civilian and didn't have nothing to do with nothing, but Live Wire had blown Ms. Diaz's head clean off of her shoulders and didn't lose a wink of sleep over it and for that reason alone Live Wire was at the top of Pauleena' s hit list.

"Nah, that motherfucker been quiet lately." Psycho told her. "But he should be popping back up soon and when he does I promise I'mma put him down." Psycho knew Live Wire was a sensitive subject, so he did his best to skate around it whenever his name popped up.

"What else been going on out there?"

"Bumped into Dice and a few Spades tonight. I don't know what's gotten into the Spades lately, but they been coming at us hard." Psycho explained. "The whole city has been a big war zone since you left."

"Don't worry about it; I'll be home in nine months." Pauleena said. "And when I get home motherfuckers is gonna wish these crackers gave ME LIFE"

"Once you come home this time we gon make sure we keep you home for good, that jail shit is for the birds."

"I heard the Gambino Brothers are back in town." Pauleena said. Word traveled fast on the inside. She knew about everything that was going on in the streets and quite frankly she didn't like how shit was playing out.

"The Gambino Brother's?"

"Yeah, these two ruthless Spanish cats." Pauleena said. "The most ruthless and brutal stick up kids to ever walk the streets and word is them motherfuckers is back in town."

"Word? That's crazy you said that cause I think Bobby Dread and his *little friend.* Had a few words with those two brothers tonight and that club." Psycho said speaking in codes not wanting to say too much on jail phone. "I'll fill you in with the rest of the story when I see you."

"You watch out for the Gambino Brothers, them fools ain't nothing to play with and when they come, they come correct. I remember this one time...."

Psycho heard a loud commotion on the other end of the phone, then suddenly the line went dead. He didn't know what happened or what was going on, he just hoped and prayed that Pauleena was alright.

Chapter Ten

Phone Check

Remy sat at a table along with three other chicks enjoying a game of Poker. Her body may have been at the Poker table, but her mind was on Pauleena. Remy watched from the corner of her eye as Pauleena used the phone. Since Remy had been playing cards she noticed that Pauleena had been on the phone for at least an hour and a half and a few of the other inmates were beginning to whisper and complain about the long length of time Pauleena was on the phone for.

Remy had been Pauleena' s cell mate going on four months now and still wasn't able to get Pauleena to open up not even a little bit. Infiltrating Pauleena's operations was a task that Remy was finally realizing wasn't as easy as she thought it would be. She had to figure out a way to get on Pauleena' s good side and not seem like she was up to something or trying to be sneaky.

The four moths of being locked up in federal prison was a mental strain on Remy. Four months was killing her and she couldn't imagine how some people spent years and the rest of their lives in a place like this. Everything about Prison was fucked up, from the food, to the nasty correctional officers, to the nosey bitches watching your every move, to a motherfucking telling you what you can and can't have, the entire situation was fucked up and after four months Remy was already sick of it.

"Yo this bitch been on the phone for wild long." A chick that went by the name Erica huffed. "I mean damn what the fuck could a motherfucker talk about for hours every day? If she think her man ain't gon go fuck other bitches cause she on the phone with him all day she bugging." She spat.

"The phone right next to Pauleena is open." Remy pointed out. "Why don't you just go and use that one?" She asked trying to stop an unnecessary altercation from happening.

"That other phone is fucked up, that bitch Pauleena is on the *good* phone and she got five minutes before I go over there and snatch her motherfucking ass up off that phone." Erica huffed as her foot began to tap involuntarily. Whoever Erica was trying to call nine times out of ten wasn't going to answer, but that wasn't the point. The truth was Erica didn't even *need* to use the phone, she was just mad that Pauleena could use the phone whenever she felt like it and that alone pissed her off.

"What's up with you and this phone shit?" Remy asked. "You don't usually be sweating the jack like that."

"Listen, I don't be using the phone like that, but when need to get on that bitch oh trust and believe I'mma get on that bitch." Erica said with much attitude.

Remy didn't say another word she just sat back and waited to see how things would play out and from the looks of things they weren't going to be good. Remy noticed Tina and a few other female Spades coming down the gallery and immediately she knew that something was about to pop off. Everyone in the jail knew about Tina and how she got down. Ever since Pauleena had beat Jessica half to death, Tina and The Spades had been quiet, Remy figured Tina and The Spades were letting a little time pass so the police would think that the beef had died down, but by the look on Tina's face

Remy could tell that something was definitely about to go down.

Once Erica spotted Tina and The Spades walking the gallery she immediately got hype as if seeing The Spades gave her the extra courage that she needed. "Yo, this bitch tripping." Erica huffed as she hopped up and headed over towards Pauleena.

"Yo!" Erica spat giving Pauleena's shoulder a forceful tap.

Pauleena spun around and gave Erica a stank look. "What!"

"I need to see that Jack." Erica's voice was hostile changing the entire vibe of the conversation.

"Ain't nobody using that phone right there." Pauleena nodded towards the phone next to her.

"That phone is fucked up." Erica said as she continued to ice grill Pauleena.

"Okay, well I'm using this phone so you gon have to wait until I finish."

"Listen." Erica began, "I ain't about to be waiting all motherfucking day to use the phone, I just *watched* you burn about five clicks, how long you expect a bitch to wait?"

"I'll be off in a minute." Pauleena said calmly, covering the receiving end of the phone so Psycho couldn't' hear the exchange. Over to her right Pauleena peeped Tina and The Spaded enter the rec area.

"Make it a second!" Erica countered giving Pauleena a look that was intended to intimidate her.

In a swift motion Pauleena turned and bust Erica upside her head with the phone knocking her out cold. "I'm over her minding…my motherfucking business…you wanna come over here with this dumb shit!" Pauleena yelled as she stood over Erica and stomped her out. "You bum ass bitches…ain't gon learn…until I murder one of y'all silly asses!"

Pauleena stopped stomping Erica out when she noticed Tina and The Spades solely begin to surround her.

Already knowing how this was going to play out Pauleena made the first move. She lunged toward Tina catching her with a stiff two piece to the face, Tina took the blows well and fired off a four punch combination of her own the only difference was Tina's punches packed a little more power. The fight went from being a strategic fight to an all out brawl. Pauleena and Tina went toe to toe and blow for blow, neither one holding anything back.

Tina threw a right cross, a punch designed and intended to knock Pauleena out. Pauleena slipped the punch and landed a left hook to Tina's temple. The punch dazed Tina and seemed to have done some damage, immediately Pauleena followed up with an eight punch combination. It looked as if she was about to finish Tina off, when out of nowhere Tina got a second wind. Tina ran into a stiff jab, then bull rushed Pauleena backwards forcing both of them to go crashing on top of the poker table, then violently down onto the floor. When the two women landed Pauleena winded up on top of Tina. Pauleena then began raining blows down onto Tina's exposed face Pauleena turning it into a bloody mess.

While the fight was going on a Spade member crept up on Pauleena from behind and stole on her.

The punch rocked Pauleena's head to the side, then another punch violently jerked her head back to the other side, then Pauleena felt punches and kicks coming from all different angles. She knew it would only be a matter of time before The Spades jumped into the fight. At the moment all Pauleena could do was ball up in a fetal position and wait for someone to come and get The Spades off of her.

Remy stood over in the cut watching the madness play out right before her eyes. It was shit like this that she thought only happened in movies, but here she was witnessing it live and in person. She had never seen *women* act like such animals before in her life.

Remy knew that this would be her only chance to prove to Pauleena that she had her back and could be trusted. She knew ahead of time the type of Shit Pauleena was into. To read it in a file was one thing, but to see it up close and in person was a whole different story.

"Here we go." Remy sighed. She picked up a chair and violently crashed it over top one of the girl's heads and watched her crumble down to the floor, blood instantly beginning to leak from her skull.

Remy then removed a tooth brush from her pocket; she had spent all night sharpening the plastic on the ground until it was pointy enough to be used as a weapon. She stabbed several Spade chicks and sliced away at the rest of them. Once all the other chicks saw that Remy held a shank in her hand they all began to scatter not wanting to be on the receiving end of the homemade knife.

Tina quickly got up off the ground and stared Remy down. "You just made a big mistake." She growled.

"Yo Rosco coming!" (Police) An inmate who was serving as a look out yelled.

Immediately Tina led The Spades over to the other side of the room while Remy helped Pauleena back up to her feet.

"Good looking back there. I appreciate that." Pauleena said doing her best to quickly fix her ponytail to make it look like she wasn't fighting.

"It's nothing." Remy said coolly. "Can't let them bitches jump my bunkie like that." Remy knew that this was the first step in earning Pauleena' s trust, she also knew that for the next few days the entire jail would be buzzing about the rumble that had just taken place and that her participation had now placed a big bull's eye on her back. Every Spade member in the jail would now be after her and she knew it.

"Don't worry about them Spade bitches, I ain't gon let them violate you." Pauleena whispered as if she could read Remy's mind. She knew that a lot of the other females in the jail were afraid to stand their ground when it came to The Spades, especially since there were so many of them, but Pauleena could care less how many of them there were, she was beginning to hate The Spades more than she hated the police.

"So what do we do from here?" Remy asked with a nervous look on her face. This was the first time she had ever stabbed or cut a person in her life, her back was drenched in sweat and her heart felt like it was about to beat out of her chest. Remy did what she had to do, but on the other end she knew there were consequences for every action.

From across the room Remy and Pauleena had an intense stare down with The Spades, as a scrawny, frail looking white C.O. patrolled the area making sure the rules and regulations were being followed by all inmates.

Pauleena smiled. "We go to war."

Chapter Eleven

Hard Lesson and Tough Choices

Dice sat at the mini bar section of his home enjoying a strong drink. Being the leader of such a powerful organization was beginning to become a bit draining as well as confusing. Dice didn't like the space that the Spades were in. The organization wasn't put together to be going to war, the organization was designed to help the communities and the people in those communities, to create jobs and give back to the people. What The Spades were turning into now was a gang. The Spades no longer created jobs for the people and they also stopped policing the communities.

On the inside Dice felt like a complete failure and loser. He knew if Wolf could see him now he would be disappointed in him, maybe even ashamed of him. There was no way Wolf would have let The Spades get to an all time low like this.

Instead of drinking from a glass like a normal person, Dice decided to guzzle straight from the bottle. For the past few days he had turned into a heavy drinker and stress was becoming his new best friend, not to mention Tonya was beginning to work his last nerves. For some strange reason Dice felt like he could no longer trust Tonya anymore, it was as if she was resorting back to the *old* Tonya and her old ways.

He was still embarrassed about how Tonya had made him out to look like a fool at the club in front of The Spades. As Dice sat at the counter getting his drink on he heard his cell phone ping notifying him that an email had just come through. He wasn't really in the mood to be answering emails, but something told him, to just check it.

Dice looked down at the phone and his eyes instantly lit up when he saw that he had received an email from Wolf.

"Damn, speaking of the devil." Dice thought as he opened the email and began to read...

From: Wolf
Subject: The Spades
Date: August 18, 2014
To: Dice
Long time no hear. How you been holding up out there? Is the movement still moving?"

Dice almost instantly hit the reply button

From: Dice
Subject: Hard times...
Date: August 18, 2014
To: Wolf
I ain't even gon lie to you big bro, things been a little rough out here. I've been having a difficult time keeping

things in order out here as of late....I hate to say this, but maybe you were wrong about me. Maybe I'm not mentally strong enough to run an organization of this magnitude and maybe I'll never be able to fill such big shoes....maybe I'm not the man you thought I was.

From: Wolf
Subject: Nonsense
Date: August 18, 2014
To: Dice

That's nonsense....Dice out of thousands of Spade members I chose you to be their leader and trust and believe I wouldn't of personally handpicked you for the job if I "thought" for one second that you weren't the man for the job... I chose you for a reason figure out the reason and be the leader that I know you are capable of being, The Spades are the future and you my friend hold the future in the palm of your hands :) I gotta run and take Ivy to the store to grab a few things; can you believe that she's six months pregnant already? And her stomach looks like it's ready to explode at any second lol....whenever you need to holla at me, just know that I am here for you....

After reading Wolf's email all Dice could do was smile. Just to know that Wolf had so much faith in him made Dice feel as if he was the right man to be running The Spades. From here on out he vowed to get things right and get The Spades back on the right track.

Dice took a swig from his bottle when he notice Tonya coming downstairs wearing a red silk robe that was left wide open exposing her naked body and a scarf tied around her head.

"You ain't hear me calling you?" Tonya asked. Her eyes went from Dice down to the bottle that rested in his hand. "Oh, no wonder you couldn't hear me, cause you down here with your new best friend." She nodded towards the bottle.

Dice shot Tonya a nasty look, but didn't say nothing. He wasn't in the mood to be arguing or fussing with her about some dumb shit so he decided to just let her ramble.

"You don't hear me talking to you?"

"What do you want Tonya?" Dice asked as if talking to her was draining him of all of his energy.

"What time you coming upstairs?"

"In a little while."

"But I want you to come now." Tonya whined. "*She* misses you." She said rubbing two fingers in a circular motion against her clit.

Dice's eyes diverted from Tonya's face, down to her hands, he then looked back up at her with a look of disgust on his face. "Nah, I'm good." he said turning the bottle up to his lips. He was sick and tired of Tonya and her bullshit, if it wasn't one thing with her then it was another.

"What you mean you good?" Tonya echoed the look of embarrassment etched on her face. "Oh so now this pussy ain't good enough for you no more?"

"Obviously it's good enough for the whole world, because you damn sure giving out samples."

Tonya sucked her teeth. "Here we go with this whole world shit." She was the type of person who knew they were dead wrong, but would still argue you tooth and nail as if they were right. "Well maybe if you spent more time at home where you *belong*, then maybe you would be able to sample your own product instead of me giving it away."

Before Tonya could even figure out what was going on, her head forcefully jerked back and blood instantly filled her mouth. Dice had smacked the shit out of her so fast she thought she was dreaming, until she raised her fingers up to her mouth and they came away bloody.

"What you hit me for?"

"Get the fuck out my house. You ungrateful bitch!" Dice growled. "I should of left you on the hoe stroll where I found ya stupid ass! I should of known you'd never change. Once a hoe, always a hoe."

"Changed!?" Tonya yelled. "You've changed Dice, not me. You! Ever since you took me back I've been nothing but good to you, you *used* to have time for me, you *used* to care about my feelings, you *used* to at least try and act like you gave a fuck about me, you *used* to talk to me like I was a human being and not a piece of trash, you *used* to love me and you never *used* to put your hands on me, but I'm the one who's changed right? No, Dice you the one who changed. Ever since you started running The Spades your attitude and your entire vibe has changed!"

Dice took a long swig from his bottle and didn't say a word, just continued to listen.

"When you took me in I changed everything for you Dice, because back then the way you cared about and treated me was like no other, but now you could care less if I came or went." Tonya said as tears poured down her face, *real* tears, not the usual fake ones. "If I walked out that door right now would you even try to stop me? Huh? Would you even care? Or better yet do you even care?"

Dice placed the bottle up to his lips and stared at Tonya as if she was retarded not saying a word. She was such a good actor, Dice couldn't tell if her words were genuine or not, wasn't able to decipher the truth from a lie, facts from bullshit, so instead he decided to play it safe and just said nothing.

"Just as I thought, you ain't got shit to say huh?" Tonya said with her arms folded across her chest. "You know what? Fuck you Dice." She said, then stormed right back up the stairs disappearing out of Dice's sight.

Dice continued to swig from his bottle as the sound of loud movement came from upstairs. The sound of things being broken could be heard followed by the sound of glass shattering. Dice figured Tonya was upstairs going crazy, destroying anything of value. As the rumbling up above continued Dice heard the door bell ring. Him and Tonya never had guest over so someone ringing his doorbell was strange, especially at this time of night.

Dice grabbed his .38 from off the counter and headed over to the door to see who in their right mind would be ringing his door bell at such a late hour. Dice looked through the peep hole and breathed a sigh of relief when he saw who was on the other side of the door. He opened the door and in stepped The Big Show followed by three Spade members.

"What's good my nigga. I don't mean to pop up like this, but we need to talk." The Big Show said looking around the house. He wore black boots, black jeans and a black cone head hoodie that covered his head and one of his gloved hands remained inside the pocket of his hoodie.

"What's on ya mind?" Dice asked leading the men over to the bar area where he poured each man a drink.

"Well it's like this." The Big Show began, "A few Spades been whispering in my ear and they not happy with the way you've been running the organization."

"Fuck them and what they think!" Dice barked. "If they got a problem with me being in charge, tell em to go take that up with Wolf"

"Wolf ain't here no more Dice." The Big Show told him. "And quite frankly Wolf has no say so what so ever right now."

Dice looked at The Big Show like her had just witnessed him smoking crack. "The nerve of you." Dice shook his head. "Wolf put this entire thing together and if it wasn't for him we'd *all* still be broke including you so how does the man who made all this possible have no say so in the situation, when he's the one who created a situation for us to begin with?"

"Wolf left us all for dead." The big Show said. "He ain't never coming back. Pauleena and her team out there getting money, Live Wire and The Real Spades out there getting money and what we doing? Sitting around looking stupid." He said answering his own question." It's time for a change."

"What you mean by that?" Dice asked with a raised eyebrow. From the look on The Big Show's face Dice could tell that he was on some grease ball shit.

"What I mean by that is you've been voted out as the leader and I've been voted in." The Big Show said with a smile.

"Does Wolf know about this?"

"Fuck Wolf!" The Big Show barked removing a chrome .357 from the pocket of his hoodie and aiming it at Dice's head, while the rest of The Spades followed his lead. "And fuck you too Dice. You ain't strong enough to lead this movement."

"You know when Wolf finds out about this he's going to have your head right?" Dice said in a matter of fact tone.

"Nigga!" The Big Show shouted, "Say Wolf name again!" He threatened. Wolf was gone and never coming back and Dice wasn't mentally strong enough to lead The Spades, so The Big Show took it upon himself to over throw him. Too many of the Spades were beginning to complain about their financial situations, so The Big Show knew he had to step in and feed the dogs before they turned around and tried to eat the food off of his plate.

The sound of another person coming down the stairs stole The Big Show's attention for a second.

"And don't think for one second that you gon be having all your bitches around my son, cause if I find out..." Tonya's words got caught in her throat when she saw several men dressed in all black aiming guns at Dice. She held her duffle bag that was filled with all of her belongings with a look of confusion on her face. "Is everything alright down here Dice?"

"Run!!" Dice yelled as the sound of multiple shots being fired could be heard. The three Spades members took off upstairs after Tonya, while The Big Show kept Dice still with the .357 aimed at his head.

"Why are you doing this?" Dice asked as several gunshots could be heard coming from upstairs.

"Because I can." The Big Show said, then pulled the trigger.

Boom!

Dice's lifeless body toppled over face first down to the floor. The Big Show stood over Dice and watched as blood leaked out of the gaping hole where Dice's head used to be. "How the fuck you gon control an organization like The Spades when you can't even control your bitch?" The Big Show said out loud as if Dice could hear him.

With Dice now finally out of the way The Spades now belonged to The Big Show and now he could start putting the pieces of his plan together. He was tired of sitting on the sideline watching everyone else ball, now it was his turn.

The Big Show watched as the three Spade members made their way back downstairs with silly looks on their faces. "What happened?"

"She got away." The tallest out of the three Spades answered.

"How the fuck did that happen?"

"Bitch ran and jumped out the window on some *"I'm gonna get you sucker"* shit."

The man standing before The Big Show explained.

"Aight put the word out that I want that bitch dead in the next 24 hours." The Big Show ordered. He was in charge and he was about to show the streets that there was a new boss in town. A boss that wasn't to be fucked with.

Chapter Twelve

I Love You

Wolf stepped out the shower; a towel wrapped around his waist was the only thing that covered him. He entered the bedroom and saw Ivy laying on her back butt naked with an erotica novel in her hand. From the looks of things he could tell that she was really into whatever she was reading, so he purposely walked over and snatched the book from her hands and began to glance through a few of the pages. "So, this what you over here clouding your brain with?" Wolf asking sitting the book down on the dresser.

"A little erotica ain't never hurt nobody." Ivy countered. "Besides those characters in the book be doing a whoooole lot of freaky shit." She said with a devilish smile.

"Why read that bullshit when you got the real thing right here?" Wolf said letting the towel drop down from his waist as he slid on the bed alongside Ivy and her big swollen belly. He made her get on all fours, then slapped her ass with force, then slapped it again just to watch it jiggle. Wolf reached his hand under Ivy's thighs and began rubbing on her clit. Instantly he could feel Ivy's clit begin to swell as his finger became drenched in her wetness.

"You wanna sit in the bed and read them silly ass books all day?" wolf asked as his fingers began to speed up.

"No Daddy!" Ivy moaned.

"Huh?"

"I said no Daddy." Ivy moaned louder as she began to move her hips to the rhythm of Wolf's fingers. "Oh my god. You bout to make me cum already, please don't stop playing with your pussy, please don't stop." Ivy begged.

"You want me to eat this ass while I play with that pussy? Huh?" Wolf growled through clenched teeth. "Huh? That's what you want me to do?" He growled now working his fingers in a circular motion.

"Yes Daddy...that's what I want"

"Well tell me then."

"Come eat this ass Daddy." Ivy moaned. "Come eat this ass Daddy."

"I can't hear you!" Wolf slapped Ivy's ass, "Say it like you mean it!"

"Oh daddy come eat this ass, please come eat this ass, eat this ass real good for Mami please Daddy." Ivy begged.

Wolf began by placing soft kisses on Ivy's butt cheeks, the type of kisses a man would give a woman on Valentine's Day. He then slowly worked his way over to Ivy's ass crack. Wolf licked Ivy's ass nice and slow letting his tongue massage her rectum, he sexually tortured Ivy with his tongue while still working overtime on her clit with is fingers. Wolf then used his other hand and slipped two fingers inside of Ivy and slowly finger fucked her, played with her clit and continued to eat her ass all at the same time.

Greedy sounds came from Ivy, sounds that told Wolf that she was enjoying every last second of the sexual torture. Over and over she moaned loudly and the more and more Wolf continued to please her.

Wolf then turned Ivy over on her side then crept behind her, dipped to get a good angle, held her waist with a firm grip and entered her walls from behind. Wolf's thrusting was deep and steady, as he lifted one of Ivy's legs up in the air going deeper and deeper with each stroke.

"Yes Daddy, right there." Ivy moaned as she craned her neck, reached back for Wolf's face and kissed him passionately. She was loving the feeling of Wolf's dick moving in and out of her. "I'm com.....I'm coming!" Ivy screamed out loud. Her eyes were closed tight, mouth open wide, she moved her head side to side, in pain, in pleasure, sweating as if she was in hell's kitchen, sweating as if she was suffering. Her body tensed as her toes curled. She trembled as she reached her climax. An orgasm that felt like it would never end an orgasm that needed to be freed.

But Wolf was only just getting started. He flipped Ivy over onto her back, placed her feet on his shoulders, entered her walls, filling her with dick, pushed until he couldn't go any further. Ivy's pregnant pussy felt like heaven on earth to Wolf.

"Fuck me harder!" Ivy yelled. Her eyed closed, her breathing intense, her body trembling and panting.

Wolf pulled his length out to the edge, then went deep inside her again. He repeated this move over and over. He moved his hands to the bends of her knees, pushed her knees back up to the side of her head, went in and out of her so fast, so deep, his stroke long and steady.

Ivy moaned, then whispered "Harder!"

Wolf fucked Ivy as hard as he could without hurting her or the baby, he felt sweat gathering on his neck, fucked her the way she kept telling his to fuck her. He kissed Ivy, did that to shut her up, that one kiss leading to so much more.

Wolf kissed Ivy's body, sucked her toes, rubbed and squeezed her ass, tasted her, licked her provocatively, licked her like she was melting ice cream forcing her to cum for him yet again.

"Get over here!" Wolf growled as he crawled over towards Ivy, straddled her face and began to fuck Ivy's mouth like there was no tomorrow. The sound of Ivy's mouth was wet, super wet and loud. Wolf plowed in and out of Ivy's mouth at a fast aggressive pace. All that could be heard throughout the house was the sound of loud moans and loud wet sucking noises.

As Wolf continued to fuck Ivy's mouth, she began to gag a bit on his length as her eyes began to tear up, but Wolf ignored Ivy's watery eyes and continued to fuck Ivy's mouth as if he was fucking a pussy.

"No you gon take this dick." Wolf growled as he continued to feed Ivy dick. He purposely pushed his dick further down her throat forcing her gag loudly. "Yeah that's right baby take this dick." Wolf grabbed two hand fulls of Ivy's hair, closed his eyes tight as his orgasm took over. "Arrrgh!" he grunted as he came all in Ivy's mouth. And like a good girl. Ivy continued sucking until she was *sure* that she had gotten every last drop out.

Wolf quickly rolled out the bed and headed in the bathroom to clean himself off, when he returned from the bathroom he notices Ivy spread all across the bed sleep with her mouth open looking stank. All he could do at the moment was smile. He loved Ivy to death, but he was happy that she was sleep right now because he had business that he needed to take care of.

Wolf quickly dressed in all black, grabbed his 9mm, stuck it in his waistband then headed out the door.

***

Wolf slowly cruised around the area with his 9m resting on his lap. He hadn't forgotten about what Maniac and his crew had done to him. He figured he'd let a little time pass before retaliating and what better time to retaliate than now.

As Wolf cruised through several blocks he spotted one of the guys who had stole on him from behind standing in front of a liquor store or "package store" as they called it in L.A. talking to two run down thirsty looking chicks.

Wolf pulled up in an empty parking spot, killed the lights, slipped his hoodie on his head and hopped out the whip (car).

"I'm saying thought, what y'all tryna do?" The man who stood in front of the liquor store asked the two women that stood before him.

"Blue you tripping." the darkest one out the two snapped. "What you mean what ywe tryna do, that's my cousin."

"And?" Blue said flashing a chipped tooth smile. He could care less if the two chicks who stood before him were cousins or not, he was in search of a three-some. "I mean I though y'all was tryna have some fun?"

"Yo Blue. You're a certified creep." The dark skin chick said, "We don't get down like that." She said in an unconvincing manner.

"Get down like what? I got the weed and lix (liquor) right here, let's go to my crib and chill." Blue smiled. "Stop thinking so much."

Before the dark skin chick could reply, a man wearing all black appeared out of nowhere with a gun in his hand and a hoodie pulled over his head with the strings drawn tight.

The women took off running as a loud shot rang out and they saw Blue go crashing down to the pavement clutching his shoulder.

"Maniac where can I find him?"Wolf asked standing over Blue's body.

"Please don't kill me man. I got six kids." Blue begged. "Please man don't do this."

Wolf raised his leg and brought it down hard, stomping Blue's head into the concrete. "Maniac where can I find him at?"

"He's down at the tittie bar two miles down the road." Blue told him as blood continued to spill from his shoulder at a rapid pace.

"Thanks." Wolf aimed his 9mm at Blue's forehead and pulled the trigger.

Boc!

Wolf hopped back in his car and headed in the direction of the tittie bar, until the ringing of his phone grabbed his attention. Only one person had his number, so she answered without bothering to look at the caller I.D. "Yo what's up?"

"Where are you?" Ivy asked, by the sound of her voice Wolf could tell that something was up.

"Right up the street why what's up?"

"I need you to come home right now?" Ivy told him.

"Is everything alright?"

"No everything is not alright; can you please just come home right now?"

"I'm on my way." Wolf ended the call and made a u-turn. He would have to catch up with maniac another time, right now he had to head home and make sure Ivy wasn't in any danger.

***

Wolf stormed in the house and spotted Ivy sitting on the couch with a sad look on her face.

"What happen?" Wolf pressed looking at Ivy for answers.

"Um, I got something to tell you." Ivy said trying to prolong the conversation. She hated being the one to have to give Wolf the bad news.

"Spit it out already!" Wolf barked. His patience was beginning to run thin.

"I got a call from Tonya while you were gone." Ivy said in a sad tone. "She said that someone...someone killed Dice."

Instantly Wolf's heart felt like it had sunk down into his stomach. He couldn't believe what he was hearing; there was no way that what Ivy had just told him could be possibly true. "Are you serious?"
Ivy slowly nodded her head up and down. "I'm sorry Wolf."

"Did Tonya say who killed him?" Wolf asked.

"She said it was The Big Show who killed Dice." Ivy informed him.

Instantly Wolf's mode went from being sad, too angry, to being flat out pissed off. "The Big Show?" he echoed. "You sure?"

"Yes, I'm sure." Ivy answered. She got up from the couch walked over to Wolf, placed his head down on her breast and gave him a tight hug. "I promise you everything is going to be alright, I know you want to avenge your friend's death, but me and the baby need you here with us." she whispered. "Please don't leave us Daddy, please leave that street shit back in New York. I need you, your daughter needs you, we are a family and your family needs you more than The Spades."

"I'm going to have a daughter?" Wolf asked in a light whisper.

"Yes, I just found out the other day I was waiting to surprise you." Ivy smiled. "Promise me you won't leave your family."

"The Spades are my family too." Wolf stated plainly.

Ivy grabbed Wolf's face and forced him to look at her. "I don't ever want you going back to New York again, your family isn't in New York any more, your family now lives in L.A. and I'm telling you now I am not raising this little girl that's in my stomach on my own, now promise me you gon leave that street shit alone and stay here where you belong with your family."

"I got you."

"I said promise me." Ivy said looking into Wolf's eyes.

Wolf remained quiet for a second or two as if he was in serious thought or undecided on what he wanted to do.

"Promise me." Ivy pressed. She then grabbed Wolf's hand and placed it on her swollen stomach. "No, promise *us*."

Chapter Thirteen

All Work and No Play

"You motherfuckers wanna fuck me? Okay......this what I do....this what I does....I'm built for this shit." The Terminator whispered over and over again to himself as he pounded away at the speed bag that hung in front of him. The biggest fight of his life was only a month away and for the first time in his career he was nervous and unsure. The Terminator had been fighting all his life, but for some strange reason this fight just felt different for some reason.

Mr. Wilson stood over to the side with a towel over his shoulder watching the champs every move closely. He didn't feel like his fighter should be going up in weight to fight a naturally bigger and harder hitting man, but for the love of money The Terminator decided to take the fight away.

After two weeks of studying tapes on Brutus the Russian sensation, Mr. Wilson was beginning to second guess The Terminator's decision to fight the undefeated Russian champion. On the tapes that Mr. Wilson watched he didn't see a fighter, he saw an animal, a man who love to inflict pain on his opponents, a man with unbelievable punching power, a man who could give a punch as well as take one, not to mention the rumors floating around that Brutus was juicing on steroids left Mr. Wilson with a few concerns.

"You want to get knocked out don't you?" Mr. Wilson barked as he watched The Terminator do a two step dance to the sound of Drake's voice booming through the speakers.

"What you huffing about now old man?" The Terminator said turning tof ace his trainer, "What am I don't wrong now?"

"For on, you're not focused and, two what is she doing here in the gym?" Mr. Wilson asked pointing at Lisa who sat quietly in a folding chair over on the sideline watching The Terminator train. Lisa's attire looked like the attire of a prostitute. She wore a short snug fitting strapless red dress, a pair of expensive looking red open toe sling backs with a four inch heel, with a bright red glossy lip stick to match.

For the past few months Lisa and The Terminator had been spending a lot of time with one another. Going from Bills to The Terminator was a huge upgrade there was no way that Lisa was going to fuck up the *great* situation that she was in for no one, she didn't care who didn't like it.

"What?" The Terminator asked with a smile.

"I said what is she doing here?" Mr. Wilson repeated in a firm tone of voice.

"What? That's my shorty." The Terminator said as if a half naked woman sitting around while he was supposed to be training wasn't a big deal.

"Well what the fuck is your *shorty* doing in the gym?"

"Part of my support team." The Terminator chuckled.

"Get her out of here right now or else I walk." Mr. Wilson threatened.

"Yo chill." The Terminator placed a friendly hand on Mr. Wilson's shoulder. "I only invited her over for a press conference that we have today, after today no more distraction I promise."

Mr. Wilson didn't understand how someone could take an opponent of Brutus's stature so lightly, how someone could be so nonchalant when so much was at stake. "For the first time in your career you're the underdog and you're over here taking your opponent for a joke." Mr. Wilson paused. "Boxing experts all around the world are saying there's no chance in hell that you'll even make it past the fourth round and you over hear joking around like shit is a game. Matter of fact, I'm done training you until you get focused and start taking this sport more seriously, men die in the ring all the time, but I'll be damned if I sit around and watch you get killed cause you wanna play around." He said as he turned and began to walk off.

"So you not gon train me no more for real?" The Terminator asked with panic in his voice. He knew without Mr. Wilson in his corner there would really be no chance at his winning the mega fight.

"Let your *shorty* train you." Mr. Wilson countered and walked off. "I'll meet you at the press conference." He yelled over his shoulder leaving The Terminator standing there looking stupid.

"Baby if you need me to leave that won't be a problem." Lisa said. She didn't want to leave her man's side, but at the end of the day she knew he was a fighter and fighters needed to be focused.

"Nah, you good." The Terminator waved Mr. Wilson off. "That old man will find something to complain about, when ain't shit to complain about."

"You sure?"

"Yeah, I'mma go hop in the shower then we can go head out to this press conference." The Terminator said, then headed to the shower room.

In the back of his mind he knew everything that Mr. Wilson had told him was right, he didn't need any distractions and The Terminator definitely had no business being involved or around any women during training . He knew this, but still

The Terminator did it anyway. The Terminator was a hell of a fighter, but he was about to enter a total different world and he was facing a totally different type fighter. After today The Terminator vowed to put his all into his training sessions. The entire world was whispering about him being knocked out before the fourth round by the Russian champion. The whispers upset and made The Terminator mad, but at the end of the day he knew people weren't saying he wasn't going to make it past the fourth round for no reason.

***

The Terminator entered the hotel where the press conference was being held and couldn't believe his eyes. The place was a zoo, reporter after reporter stormed the champ when he entered the building, bright lights damn near blinded The Terminator as his body guards led him through the riled up crowd of reporters, media and fight fans. The Terminator played it cool and continued to follow the path that his bodyguards had led for him.

The Terminator strolled into the press conference area shining like a million bucks. He wore all black with several expensive looking diamond chains draped around his neck, not to mention a huge pinky ring as well as a chunky bracelet on his wrist, a pair of Ray Bans covered his eyes and he had a bad bitch in a red dress by his side.

Over on the other side of the room The Terminator spotted Brutus the Russian sensation and his team posted up wearing Suits looking like professional business men.

"Clowns," The Terminator mumbled, then walked over and took a seat in front of a microphone next to Mr. Wilson. "Everything you said back there was right and I promise from now on I'mma give it 150%." He whispered in Mr. Wilson's ear.

Mr. Wilson replied with a simple head nod. "In order to beat this guy it's going to take defense, counter punching and footwork." He whispered back as the press conference began.

"Terminator, how do you plan to defeat a man like Brutus?" A reporter asked.

"Easy." The Terminator shrugged. "I'mma knock him the fuck out."

"No one else has been able to knock or even come close to knocking Brutus out, so what makes you think you'll be able to get the job done?"

"He ain't never saw a motherfucker like me before." The Terminator said in a cocky manner. "I'm a slick fighter, I have good punching power and I'm the smartest fighter he's ever been in the ring with and did I mention how handsome I am?" He flashed a smile for the camera.

"Most experts and fight analyst say they don't see you making it past the fourth round, what do you have to say about that?" A black reporter who wore a pair of thick bifocals asked.

"Fuck the so called experts; they don't know shit about shit." The Terminator said. “Anybody who thinks I won't make it past four all they gotta do is out their money up and get an easy pay day."

"Over here champ." A Chinese reporter called getting The Terminators attention. "Why did you agree to take the fight out in Russia, why not have the fight right here in America?"

"Because I wanted to go to Brutus’s back yard and whip his ass." The Terminator chuckled. And also show the clown that you can hit as hard as you want, but skills pay the bills around here."

Do you have anything you want to say to Brutus?" Another reporter asked.

"Actually I do." The Terminator said turning to face Brutus. "Next month you going night, night so bring a pillow with you." he was trying to get up under Brutus' skin and into his head. The Terminator tried not to show it, but Brutus being the favorite and him being the underdog really pissed him off.

The reporters then turned their attention over to Brutus. "Is The Terminator going to be the toughest opponent you've ever face?"

"This guy is a joke." Brutus said seriously. "I mean really, is this the best that the U.S. has to offer? I will dispose of this trash effortlessly, like taking candy from a baby."

"Do you feel like you have an advantage with the fight taking place in Russia, rather than over here in America?" The Black reporter with the bifocals asked.

"I could care less where the fight took place; the ending result would still remain the same, The Terminator getting terminated." Brutus told the room full of people.

"Man listen." The Terminator said jumping into the conversation. "After I knock this Russian motherfucker out, I'm going to take his wife out to dinner and show her what its like to be with a *real* man." He turned and looked at Brutus' wife who sat in the front row wearing an expensive looking silver gown. "Hey baby." He said, then blew her a kiss.

Brutus jumped out of his seat, but was quickly restrained by his team.

"What?" The Terminator smiled. "Don't you want your wife to be happy?" He continued to taunt.

"I'm cool." Brutus said readjusting his tie and taking his seat. "You my friend just let your big mouth get you into something that your ass ain't going to be able to get you out of." he said staring a hole through The Terminator. "Can I have everyone's attention please? I've created a video that I would like for everyone to see, especially my opponent...roll it."

A projector screen rolled down from the ceiling and the lights suddenly got dim. Seconds later Brutus's face appeared on the screen. He stood shirtless and next to him stood a full grown horse whose skin he was rubbing slowly and with affection. "Terminator in one month I'll finally be able to get my hands on you, when we're in the ring it's just going to be me and you, no one will be able to help you and no one will be able to come to your rescue. You can do all the training you want none of that is going to help you come fight night. I'm going to hurt you James. I'm going to hurt you real bad and I can't wait. Experts say you won't make it to the fourth round." Brutus chuckled, "They must like you, because I don't even see you getting out of the first round...I'm going to end this video on a more civil note." in a quick motion Brutus spun and snuffed the horse, knocking it unconscious. The punch was so swift and powerful that everyone who witnessed the video in the room jumped and gasped feeling sorry for the horse. Brutus looked directly into the camera and said, "Ready or not here I come!" That was how the video ended.

When the lights came back on the place was in an uproar, the media and fight fans were going crazy. A loud chatter filled the room as people jumped on their phones to report what they saw. The Terminator turned and looked at Mr. Wilson who wore a scared and worried look on his face. He was glad he wore dark shades that way the media and fight fans couldn't see the fear that resided in his eyes as well as his heart. *"I know this motherfucker ain't just knock out a horse."* The Terminator said to himself over and over again. The footage of his opponent knocking a horse out kept replaying over and over in his head.

"Both fighters up front for the face off." One of the promoters announces. The Terminator slowly stood up and met Brutus at the center of the stage where the two met standing face to face, only inches of space stood in between the two fighters.

"Next month you belong to me." Brutus growled through clenched teeth. "I'm going to hurt you real bad."

"I'll die before I lose to a *white boy*." The Terminator countered with a smile on his face.

The look on Brutus' face was stone and serious. One could tell that he really didn't like The Terminator, this fight wasn't business it was now personal. "This *white boy* is going to knock you out in front of the whole world."

"I feel sorry for your mother." The Terminator disrespected.

"Keep my mother's name out your mouth." Brutus growled, his hands turning into fist.

"How about I put something in her mouth." The Terminator shot back. In a flash Brutus's hand shot out and forcefully mushed The Terminator. The mush was so powerful that it snapped The Terminator’s head back and forced his shades to go flying off of his face. The Terminator answered back with a swift left hook, that Brutus managed to weave by a finger nail. Before things got a chance to get too out of control several security guards jumped in the middle and separated the two.

"I'mma kill you motherfucker!" The Terminator yelled trying to break free from security and get to Brutus.

Mr. Wilson quickly draped his arm around The Terminator’s neck and pulled him away from the spectacle. "We got four more weeks to get you prepared can you give me a hundred percent?" he whispered in his fighter's ear.

"I'mma give you a hundred and fifty percent." The Terminator replied he now realized that what he was up against wasn’t a joke nor a game. His opponent was out to seriously hurt him and embarrass him by knocking him out cold on live television and that was something that The Terminator refused to let happen. If he ain't never been focused before, he was definitely focused now more than ever.

Chapter Fourteen

You Stupid

Psycho sat in the den along with Prince, Bobby Dread, a few of Bobby Dreads wild rough looking Jamaican niggaz, as Pauleena' s army of Muslim body guards floated throughout the mansion looking for any signs of trouble.

On Psycho's lap rested a picture of Pauleena and another woman who Pauleena had told Psycho in a letter was her cell mate. Also in the letter Pauleena told Psycho that her and the girl that went by the name Remy had been getting rather close as of late and that she wanted Psycho to use the "click-click" polaroid picture of her and Remy to find out who Remy really was and if or how much of her word could be trusted.

Next to Psycho sat a folder, inside that folder was all of Remy's information as well as a graduation picture of Remy graduating from the police academy. Psycho had paid a retired detective a couple gees to acquire the information that he requested, now all he had to do was wait for Pauleena to call so he could put her on what was going on.

"Fucking pigs I can't stand these motherfuckers." Psycho spat with a disgusted look on his face as he eyed Remy's picture.

"Pauleena can handle her own." Prince said, "These crackers must want her real bad."

"Fuck them my baby is going to handle that fucking rat ass bitch." Psycho huffed. "Six more weeks and baby will be here and I can't wait."

Being as though Pauleena was coming home so soon, Psycho decided to cut Monica off for good this time. It was going on a month and a half since the last time he saw or even spoke to Monica and honestly Psycho felt good about his decision. The last thing he needed was for Pauleena to find out about his infidelity while she was away rotting in jail. She's in jail fighting to stay alive each and every day, while Psycho's on the outside living the good life doing him. Psycho knew what he was doing was wrong, but he made excuse after excuse to why he was doing what he was doing. But at the end of the day his decision to cut Monica off was the best thing he could have ever done.

Psycho glanced down at this watch, then looked up at Prince and Bobby Dread, "So how y'all feel about this Big Show nigga and The Spades coming over here to chop it up?"

"After The Big Show killed Dice and has been running things The Spades have been falling back from coming after our people," Prince pointed out. "so if he wants to talk I say let's hear him out and maybe put him up to a small test to see if what he's talking about is real or not."

"How you feel about the situation?" Psycho asked looking over at Bobby Dread.

"I don't give a fuck about The Spades anymore." Bobby Dread growled. "My main focus is now on The Gambino Brothers." Bobby Dread was still pissed about what had happened at the club and couldn't wait to run into the two brothers again.

"Nah, the Gambino Brothers are all mines!" Prince said patting his chest. Not only did one of them shoot Prince, but they also robbed him of all of his valuable possessions. Prince now had a slight limp when he walked cause of the brother that went by the name Victor. Prince placed a $15,000 bounty on The Gambino Brothers head, $15, 000 for each brother. Every goon, thug and broke nigga with a gun was out looking for The Gambino Brothers and Prince knew it would only be a matter of time before he got that call.

"Yo, it's Showtime." Psycho announced. On the security monitor he watched The Big Show and a few Spades hop out of a black van and make their way to the door.

"Thanks for taking out the time to meet with me and The Spades." The Big Show said extending his hand.

"So glad we could sit down and talk." Psycho shook The Big Show's hand. "Okay, now talk to me."

"This war of ours is unnecessary and bad for business." The Big Show began. "I tried to tell Dice to stop this silly nonsense, he wouldn't listen so I had to cancel his contract. Dice and Wolf are the two dumbest motherfuckers I ever met in my life!" He huffed, "With all these solders under The Spades umbrella, no way we can't take over each state one by one. Now that I'm in charge or running the show, The Spades are about to be known throughout the whole world." He paused. "The Spades are now down to 19,000 members strong and I know that if we were to team up with Pauleena and you guys, we'd be able to run the world. We'd be accountable for all the drugs in the streets as well as the prison system. I come in peace and ask that you consider my offer. The Spades would rather work with you than against you."

Psycho stared at The Big Show for a few seconds, then said. "How do I know I can trust you? I mean what if you try to pull a stunt like that clown Live Wire did, how can I be certain that you are a man of your word?"

"Glad you asked." The Big Show smiled, "Since trust is a thing that is earned and not given, I say how bout we do a test run for let's say the next thirty days, we come together and work as a team for thirty days, if shit don't work out then we can both go our separate ways...what do you say?"
"Give me a day or two to talk it over with my team and I'll get

back to you." Psycho told him. He didn't just want to jump head first into a situation especially with Pauleena so close to coming home. When she called him tonight he would run it by her and see what she had to say or how she felt about the proposition at hand.

Before Psycho could continue on with the conversation a loud scuffle coming from down the hallway grabbed his and everyone else in the den's attention. The sound of a woman cursing could be heard. With each curse word the volume of the woman's voice was becoming louder and louder.

"Get yo fucking hands off me motherfucker!" Monica yelled as she fought and struggled to break free of the Muslim's grip. "That's words to my mother you better let me go before I count to three!"

Psycho rushed out into the hallway to see what all the commotion was about. When he spotted Monica fighting with one of the Muslim body guards. Psycho's mood immediately went from good to pissed off. Monica struggling with the Muslim body guard looked like the scene in the movie *The Five Heartbeats* when Eddie Cane was trying to fight off security at the end of a concert to get the attention of the other heart beats. "Yo let her in." Psycho yelled.

When the Muslim bodyguard released Monica she turned and smacked the shit out of him.

Slap!

"Don't you ever put your hands on me again." Monica spat, "fucking suitcase Muslim!"

"What the fuck is you doing here?" Psycho growled. Monica had crossed the line of no return when she showed up to Pauleena's mansion. "And how the fuck did you find out where I live?"

"I know every motherfucking thing I want to know about you." Monica said as if she had out smarted Psycho by finding out him and Pauleena's address. "Didn't I tell you that if you ever tried to leave me that I'd always find you? Well here I am." She said with a smile and her arms folded across her chest. "I found you."

"What is it that you want?"

"Fuck you mean what I want?" Monica looked Psycho up and down like he was crazy, "You my man right, you my daddy right? Well here I am Daddy." She said with sarcasm in her voice. "And you lucky I didn't bring all my shit with me." She was talking so loud that it forced Prince, Bobby Dread and The Big Show to come out of the den to see what was going on.

"Please leave." Psycho asked in a calm tone. One could tell that it was taking everything inside of him not to put Monica's head through a wall.

"What the fuck you mean please leave, nigga you bugging. I've been trying to get in contact with you for over a month and a half, you ain't wanna answer my calls, so here I am....hello." She said in a dramatic fashion.

"Please leave."

"What you don't love me know more!" Monica shouted loud enough for the audience that stood around her to hear. "Word? Say that's your word, say that's your word you don't love me no more. Oh but I bet you *love me* while you tryna suck my ovaries up out this pussy or better yet I bet you *love me* when I'm sucking on that small as shit in between your legs that you call a dick, you know what I'm tired of you and all your..."

Psycho's hand shot out in a blur, he grabbed the side of Monica's head and rammed it into the wall. He was trying to be patient with her dumb ass, but he could no longer take the disrespect. Psycho followed up with a strong back hand that sat Monica on her ass, he then grabbed Monica by her hair and began dragging her towards the exit while she kicked and screamed all the way out the door.

"Bitch don’t you ever bring yo stupid ass around here again!" Psycho barked as he handed Monica over to one of the

Muslim security guards. During the hand off Monica managed to slip a kick into Psycho's mid-section.

"I'm going to kill you!" Monica yelled at the top of her lungs as she was roughly escorted out of the mansion.

Psycho stood in the hallway breathing heavy, Monica was really starting to work his last nerves, he didn't want to have to kill her, but he was afraid that Monica was going to leave him no choice. People like Monica didn't understand simple words like no.

Psycho looked up and noticed Prince, Bobby Dread and The Big Show all staring at him with judgmental looks on their faces. "What?"

Prince shook his head and said, "Nigga you stupid."

"Pauleena is going to kill you." Bobby Dread added in a serious tone.

"Pauleena ain't gon do shit cause she ain't gon find out about shit." Psycho said, his voice may have sounded confident, but on the inside he was scared shit less. He loved Pauleena with all his heart there was no denying that, but in her absence his needs still needed to be fulfilled at least that's what he told himself.

"When you lay down with dogs you're bound to get fleas." Bobby Dread said drawing laughter from Prince and The Big Show. He didn't mean what he said to be a joke or an insult, but he could tell by the look on Psycho's face that he had taken the comment the wrong way.

"Now motherfuckers wanna be comedians." Psycho spat looking Bobby Dread up and down, "Now ain't the time."

"I respect that." Bobby Dread bowed down, he knew Psycho already felt bad enough about dealing with Monica from the jump and he didn't want to make the man feel worse than he already did. "Didn't mean no disrespect."

"It's cool." Psycho gave Bobby Dread a fist bump. Now he had to figure out how to keep Pauleena from finding out about his affair with Monica, if worse came to worse he would just have to have Monica killed. Psycho didn't want to do it, but the next time Monica popped up or called his phone he was going to have her killed. Psycho hoped and prayed that Monica got the message today.

Chapter Fifteen

Yeah Right

Live Wire stood leaned up against the bar in a lounge out in Brooklyn. He didn't usually fuck with Brooklyn like that too tough, the last couple of times him and The Real Spades partied out in Brooklyn Live Wire found himself having to clap a few niggaz. But tonight was different. Tonight Live Wire was in a lounge out in Brooklyn because he was thinking about investing in the night spot and becoming part owner. A cat Live Wire did time with in the past that went by the name Mitch owned the lounge, but he was looking for a partner, one who could maybe add a little more excitement to the place and what better person to spice up his lounge then Live Wire.

"What you think about the place?" Live Wire asked Bills as he watched all the people dancing on the crowded dance floor like there was no tomorrow.

"It's aight." Bills struggled. He bobbed his head to the music that pumped through the speakers, but he also kept his eyes on the fake tough looking group of men who stood leaned up against a wall not too far from the bar area. "I mean if you invest in the joint we gon have to have the place renovated cause the type of crowd we gon bring in this place won't even be able to hold half of that." He pointed out.

"You right." Live Wire nodded his head up and down. He heard everything that Bills had said, but at the moment he was only half listening. His focus was on Sparkle. She stood in the middle of the dance floor with one of her home girls doing the type of dancing that women did in a gentlemens clubs and after hour spots. Sparkle wore a red Tarzan type of shirt that strapped around only one shoulder, her large breast threatened to spill out of the tight fitting shirt at any given moment. Down low she wore a pair of red Good2Go leggings and a pair of red open toe shoes with a nice heel covering her feet.

As Live Wire watched Sparkle it seemed to him as if her already huge fake ass was getting bigger. The red leggings she wore looked as if they were having a hard time containing all that ass. Men of all shapes and sizes gawked at and openly flirted with Sparkle and that was beginning to piss Live Wire off. Yeah he had plenty of women, but Sparkle was his main joint and he didn't play when it came to her. They were both two jealous time bombs waiting to explode.

"What's up with Lisa?" Live Wire asked trying to take his mind off of Sparkle. "You heard from her lately?"

"Nah." Bills said, "Last I hear she was fucking with The Terminator." He said with a hint of jealousy in his voice.

"Who that boxing nigga?"

"Yeah, that clown."

"Yea, he fight this brolic Russian cat in a few days. I saw a video on World Star where the Russian nigga knocked out a horse." Live Wire announced.

"A horse?"

"Yeah a horse." Live Wire reported. "I'mma bet $100,000 on that Russian kid." Just as the words left Live Wire's mouth he spotted a familiar face enter the lounge and begin to head straight towards him.

The chick with blue eyes stopped directly in front of Live Wire with her team of bodyguards flanked closely behind her. "So, it's like that?" the chick with the blue eyes huffed. "You can't return my calls?"

"I been busy Tori." Live Wire said in a dry tone. He and Tori or the Madam as everyone else called her had been dealing with one another for quite a while, the problem was The Madam had begun to get too attached to Live Wire and tried to begin to control him and tell him what he should and shouldn't be doing, so in return Live Wire slowly began to cut her off. Tori was a good woman, she just wasn't good enough for Live Wire.

"You been too busy to answer your phone or reply back to one of my text messages just to let me know you were okay?" Tori yelled. "I was worried sick about you; I thought something had happened to you."

"You right."

"Do you even love me? Huh?" Tori asked with pain and hurt in her eyes. "You promised me all these beautiful things and haven't delivered on one promise yet, not one"

"You right."

"Have you even thought about moving to Texas with me like you promised you would?"

Live Wire looked at Tori for a few second and said, "You right."

"I'm right about what?" Tori yelled. Live Wire's nonchalant attitude was beginning to piss her the fuck off. "You wanna play these mind games with me and keep saying I'm right cause you dead wrong and ain't got shit to say."

"You right." He said again causing Bills to erupt with laughter.

"Say I'm right again and watch me rip your head off in this whack ass hole in the wall club." Tori barked.

"How did you even find me anyway?" Live Wire asked lifting the bottle of Ciroc he held in his hand up to his lips and took a swig. "What you stalking me now. Let me find out." He said as him and Bills enjoyed another laugh.

"Everything is a joke to you." Tori said, as tears streamed down her cheek. "I love you Live Wire regardless of how bad you treat me. I love you and that's something that ain't going to ever change, I'm going to leave you alone now, but if you ever need me please know I'm only a call away."

"You right"

That was the last straw. Tori could no longer take Live Wire's disrespect. It wasn't the disrespect that hurt Tori, but the fat that Live Wire didn't even care, was what hurt the most.

Tori swung and tried to slap the shit out of Live Wire, but he was on point and easily weaved the blow.

"Yo you better chill the fuck out." Live Wire warned. His hands were bisexual, meaning he didn't care if it were a man or woman if you violated he was putting hands on you, point blank period.

"I better or what?" Tori challenged, she was already turned up to the point of no return.

Before Live Wire got a chance to reply Sparkle and her home girl Latoya popped up on the scene.

Sparkle cleared her throat letting her presence be known. "Somebody got a problem with they hands over here?" she asked giving Tori a stank look.

Tori gave Sparkle a once over and wasn't impressed. "Oh, so this why you ain't been answering your phone?" Tori yelled. "This who you been playing house with?"

"Playing house?" Sparkle echoed, "Bitch you sound stupid. Playing house, no boo boo this is home. I am where home is." She pulled a set of keys out of her purse and dangled them in Tori's face. "I have keys to *our* house, I'm his Queen, you ain't nothing but *one* of his side bitches!"

Sparkle's words cut through Tori like a knife, she knew Live Wire was out doing his thing, but to see one of the women he was dealing with up close and in person was a different story. Tori loved Live Wire to death and for him to let the woman before him speak to her like that was saying a whole lot. Tori then took a second to glance down at Sparkle's jumbo sized ass, she knew Live Wire was an ass man and she also knew she'd never be stacked like that in that department, and that alone hurt her ego.

"You know what." Tori said in a hurt tone. "I'mma leave you alone so you and your hood rat can live happily ever after. Fuck you Live Wire you ain't shit." As Tori went to walk off Latoya tried to steal on her from the side, but one of The Madam's body guards caught Latoya fist before the blow got a chance to land and roughly shoved her down to the floor. From there all hell broke loose.

Waka Flocka's voice banged through the speakers and had the entire lounge bouncing all over the place.

Bills swooped in and snuffed the body guard who had shoved Latoya down to the floor, another body guard called himself jumping into the mix, but several of The Real Spades were on him like a pack of wolves.

Sparkle tossed a drink in Tori's face before the rest of her body guards quickly escorted her out of the club and out of harm's way.

Once The Real Spades finished beating the two body guards to a pulp, Live Wire and his team headed outside. He had love for Tori and all that, but he didn't like how her team of security was tryna front like they was really bout that life, he was about to show them the meaning of the word gansta.

Live Wire stepped outside and before he got a chance to do anything, he felt a hard slap to the back of his head.

Pop!

Live Wire spun around and saw Sparkle in front of him with her arms folded across her chest and a mean look on her face.

"What?" he asked as if he didn't know what the slap was for.

"You fucked her didn't you?"

"Huh?"

"Huh, my ass. That nasty ass white girl. You fucked her didn't you?" Sparkle repeated the question, this time with a little more attitude.

"You wilding right now." Live Wire said still not answering the question. He was the best at not answering questions and flipping the script making it seem like he was the victim, instead of it being the other way around. "I don't even know that girl."

"Yo stop playing with me!" Sparkle growled biting down on her bottom lip. "Stop lying all the time, how the fuck you don't know that girl?"

"I don't!"Live Wire said sticking to his story. There was no way he was going to tell on himself....where they do that at?

"Yeah, you don't know her, but she sure as hell *knows* you." Sparkle huffed, "Did you eat her pussy?"

"Yo listen, I ain't got time for all this back and forth shit, either love me or leave me alone, which one you gon do?" Live Wire's voice boomed.

"Love you." Sparkle said in a voice just above a whisper.

"I can't hear you!"

"I said love you." Sparkle said as she melted in Live Wire's arms and rested her head on his chest as tears fell from her eyes. She knew Live Wire was no good and couldn't keep his dick in his pants to save his life and most of the time he was mean and nasty to her. Sparkle also knew that Live Wire wasn't never going to change; he was a product of the streets, a product of a fast life and a product of his environment. At the end of the day Live Wire could be all of those things, but the fact still remained that whatever Live Wire was he was all hers and Sparkle loved him to death and wouldn't trade him for anything in the world.

"Can you at least try to be good and not sleep with every woman that has a fat ass?" Sparkle asked while still wrapped in Live Wire's arms.

"I'll think about it." Live Wire said slyly as he looked up and spotted Agent Starks and four other men dressed in jeans and baseball jersey's a clear give away that they were indeed cops. "Fuck this pig want now?" Live Wire mumbled.

A few of The Real Spaded went and blocked the agent's path, to give Live Wire time to do what he needed to do.

Live Wire was just about to hand his .45off to Sparkle, so she could stash it when he saw Agent Starks pull out his hammer (gun) and blow one of The Real Spades members head clean off his shoulders. The rest of the agents quickly followed Agent Starks lead and opened fire on the group of men.

Live Wire quickly sent several shots in the agent's direction, as he grabbed Sparkle's hand and quickly tried to get her out of the line of fire. "Come on, we out!" He yelled pulling Sparkle along. Sparkle quickly kicked off her heels and ran bare foot on the concrete in order to keep up with Live Wire.

Live Wire fired a few more reckless shots over his shoulder, as he hopped in the passenger seat of Sparkle's Benz truck. Sparkle hopped behind the wheel and peeled out of the parking lot as The Real Spades continued to shoot it out with Agent Starks and the rest of the agents.

A million thoughts ran through Live Wire's mind, he had never seen agents open fire like that without a warning, especially out in an open space like that. Live Wire didn't know what was going on, but the next time a cop tried to roll up on him, he was going to shoot first and ask questions later.

Chapter Sixteen

No Turning Back

The Terminator and Mr. Wilson hopped off the plane in Russia, surrounded by a fleet of security. Russian fight fans as well as the media had been lined up for hours waiting for The Terminator's arrival. The big fight was only two days away and The Terminator was as ready as he was going to be. After the press conference he and Mr. Wilson went back and watched every last one of Brutus's fights. Mr. Wilson had pointed out the Russian's flaws and created a blue print on how The Terminator would beat the undefeated champ.

The Terminator and Mr. Wilson stepped foot out of the terminal and was met by wild drunken, American hating fight fans along with the media. Immediately fight fans began yelling, cursing and disrespecting The Terminator. The terminator noticed several of the fight fans held Russian flags in the air and waved them back and forth all while yelling and screaming at the top of their lungs.

"Fuck you, you American monkey!" One fan yelled,

"Somebody kill that nigger!" Another fan screamed as he tried to attack The Terminator, but was quickly taken down by a team of security.

"Brutus is going to kill you!"

"I hate you American scum!"

"Brutus is going to send your nigger ass back to America in a body bag one fan yelled, then spat in The Terminator's face.

Once outside The Terminator was quickly rushed in the back seat of an awaiting S.U.V. Before the S.U.V. could even pull away from the cord, The Terminator was furious. "These racist Russian motherfuckers gon make me kill one of they dumb assess!"

"Stay focused." Mr. Wilson replied quickly. "We ain't come here for that, we came here to go to work." he reminded his fighter. "Whatever you upset about take it out on Brutus come fight night."

The Terminator knew what Mr. Wilson was saying was right so for the rest of the ride he just remained silent and kept his thoughts to himself, in less than 48 hours he would be in the fight of his life and knew he didn't have time to be worrying or dwelling on foolishness. All the bullshit that The Terminator had to deal with just made him want to get in the ring with Brutus even quicker. He couldn't wait to get his hands on the so called champ; in 48 hours somebody was going to get hurt, the question was who?

Chapter Seventeen

New Life

Wolf sat in the hospital holding his newborn daughter in his arms. Ivy had given birth to a beautiful baby girl in the middle of the night, after being in labor for over ten hours and having a natural birth she was drained to the maximum mentally as well as physically.

All the pain and suffering was well worth it when Ivy looked up and saw Wolf holding his daughter in his arms while the little princess slept.

Even if Wolf wanted to, there was no way he could get the smile that was on his face to be removed. After seeing his daughter born Wolf vowed to change his life as well as his way of thinking. Ivy and little Sunshine was Wolf's only family now, the Spades were now a closed chapter in Wolf's life, he could no longer live for them, but instead he had to start living for his new family.

"I love you sooooooo much." Ivy said, she was looking a little rough and beat down, but she was still alive. "Y'all look so cute."

"You look a hot mess." Wolf joked.

"You stuck with me, so what you see is what you get." Ivy said. "I wouldn't let you leave even if you tried,"

"There you go with that crazy talk again." Wolf shook his head. When Ivy was in the eight and nine month stages of her pregnancy, she finally agreed to let Wolf get them a bigger place. Ivy had told Wolf not to go overboard, but of course he had over done it, like she knew he would.

Wolf went out and brought them a brand new five bedroom, three level house, with a four car garage. He had spent a pretty penny on their home, but he had more than enough money to spare, so he figured why not buy a comfortable home for him and his family to live in.

Two weeks ago Wolf had received information that Tonya had been murdered by the Spades. She took twelve shots to the body, then was set on fire. Ever since The Big Show had taken over The Spades, he had turned them from an organization out to help and rebuild the community, to an army who was programmed to kill and get money. The Big Show and The Spades had been taking over vacant territory block by block at a rather quick pace and with Pauleena backing him there was no telling how far he would take things.

When Wolf first received the information about Tonya and what The Big Show was out there doing he became furious and instantly wanted to take matters into his own hands, but holding his daughter in his arms made him realize that something's that he used to think were so important no longer mattered, the only thing that mattered to him now was Ivy and little Sunshine. Wolf named his daughter Sunshine because his whole life had been filled with hard times, struggling and being broke. His entire life had been dark and gloomy, but now his life felt so bright, he felt like a new man and he thanked god for giving him a second chance at life, the little girl in his arms brightened up his life so much that it was only right that he named his daughter Sunshine.

"What you over there thinking about?" Ivy asked looking over at Wolf.

"I want to get married and do the family thing the right way." Wolf said seriously. If he was going to do this, he figured why not do it right, there was nothing in this world that Ivy and little Sunshine couldn't have while he was living on the earth.

"Don’t gas me up like that."

"Nah, I'm dead ass." Wolf said seriously. He was ready to go all the way with Ivy, he had been with plenty of women in his day, but none of them even came close to comparing to Ivy in anyway, the love she had for him couldn't be duplicated or ever matched if you combined ten women and put them all together. "Will you marry me?" Wolf asked holding little Sunshine in his arms.

Ivy smiled from ear to ear. "Yes of course I will marry you."

Chapter Eighteen

I'm going To Kill You

Pauleena sat posted up leaning against the wall on the phone. She couldn't believe what Psycho was telling her on the other line, the more she listened the more angrier she felt herself becoming and the more she wanted to kill someone. "Say word. Aight bet say no more. I love you too." Pauleena said, and then hung up the phone. She was furious at what she had just found out on the phone. Psycho had just informed Pauleena on the research he'd done on Remy or Agent Smith according to her files. If it was one thing Pauleena hated was being played for a fool. Out of all the things Remy could be, she had to be a cop, a pig, a coward who hid behind a badge and for trying to play Pauleena, Remy's life was now on a countdown.

Pauleena walked in the day room and helped herself to a seat over in the corner. She made sure she placed her back to the wall so she could observe her surroundings and see who came or left the day room. On T.V. screen was an episode of

"Love and Hip Hop" most of the girls in the jail would gather around the T.V. every Monday and enjoy the on screen drama.

Pauleena sat enjoying the show, when the constant sound of dominoes being slammed down on the table followed by loud cursing could be heard making it difficult to hear the T.V.. Pauleena glanced back at the table, and noticed four women in the middle of a shit talking competition.

"Yo!" Pauleena yelled grabbing the four girls at the back table's attention. "We tryna hear the T.V. up here."

"Fuck that got to do with us?" An ugly fat girl who wore a nappy afro and had one gold tooth in her mouth spat. "This ain't Pauleena's day room; the day room is for everybody, what you think you special or something….fuck outta here!"

"Ain't nobody say nothing about being special, all I'm asking is that y'all keep it down a little bit so we can hear the T.V." Pauleena said in a calm tone. Now that she was short and so close to going home she'd notice a few inmates that used to be church houses now talking to her like they were tough. Pauleena was trying her hardest to keep her nose clean and stay out of trouble, all she had left was two more weeks, fourteen days and she was out the door a free woman. But it seemed like the closer she made it to freedom, the more she was being tested.

"Keep it down?" Ugly repeated with a stank look on her face. "You must got me fucked up." She purposely said loud for everyone in the dayroom to hear.

"Why is y'all even playing dominoes when you see other people tryna watch T.V. anyway?"

"Listen bitch." Ugly barked, "If you don't like people making noise while you watching T.V. then don't come to jail,"

The more the ugly bitch spoke the angrier Pauleena was becoming, she wasn't used to taking disrespect from no one, but taking it from an ugly bitch made it seem ten times worse. Not to mention Pauleena knew the ugly girl was only fronting because she knew she had an audience.

"Listen all I'm asking for is a little courtesy , y'all back there making wild noises and y'all probably ain't even play for no money and all that tough toney shit you back there talking you and I both know you ain't even like that so knock it off before I get upset." Pauleena said. She was two seconds from putting blood in the ugly bitch's mouth.

"You bitches kill me." Ugly said shaking her head. "Get ready to go home and now niggaz wanna be tough, like who you think you fooling? Stop playing with me little girl before I smack the shit outta you."

Before the words even left the ugly bitch's mouth, Pauleena was already on her feet heading in her direction. She knew she only had a few days left to go, but some things just had to be addressed and some people just weren't happy until something happened to them. Before Pauleena, got a chance to reach the ugly bitch, Remy stepped in front of Pauleena.

"It ain't worth it." Remy whispered in Pauleena's ear, then escorted her out of the day room. As Pauleena was exiting the day room, the ugly bitch began popping even more shit since she knew the chance of things getting physical were slim to none, now that Remy was restraining Pauleena.

"Tired of these bum ass bitches." Pauleena huffed as her and Remy made their way back to their cell. Pauleena lay on her bunk, while Remy climbed and hopped up on the top bunk.

"Fuck them bitches. In two weeks you gon be free." Remy said from the top bunk. "Think about all the money that's out there waiting for you."

"When you go home again?" Pauleena asked removing her homemade knife from up under her pillow and eyeing it carefully. Never in her life would she have expected her cell mate to be an undercover agent. Pauleena had to admit, Remy played the role of an inmate well. Pauleena had witnessed Remy curse the police out, fight with a few of the other inmates , she had even seen her cut a few chicks, now to find out she was a cop fucked her head up.

“I go home three weeks after you.” Remy said. “We should hook up in the streets.” She said throwing it out there to see if Pauleena would bite the bait. “Introduce me to your people’s. I’ll introduce you to my people’s and get this money.”

“What you locked up for anyway?” Pauleena asked just to see how far Remy was willing to go with her lies.

“I was out in Ohio doing my thing, when one of them jealous ass country niggaz snitched on me, luckily for me when the police raided my crib all they found were a couple of bullets in my crib.” Remy explained.

“You had a connect in Ohio?”

“Best connect ever, prices dirt cheap. I think he was getting em fresh off the boat.”

“Yeah?” Pauleena asked. The more Remy lied the more it was beginning to piss Pauleena off and the more she wanted to stab Remy right there in the cell, but Pauleena knew she would have to be smart about the situation especially since she had only had a few days left until she would be released.

“Word. We should link up when we get to the town.” Remy suggested as her and Pauleena’s cell cracked open.

“On the chow!” They could hear the police on the loud speaker announce.

“What they got for chow?” Pauleena asked as she sat up and slipped the shank down into her pocket.

“I think pizza.” Remy said. “You fucking wit it?”

“Yeah, fuck it why not I’ll come take the walk with you,” Pauleena said as her and Remy exited their cell and headed down to the mess hall. For the entire walk to the Mess hall Pauleena thought about taking Remy’s head off for her deceitful ways. Out of all things Remy turned out to be a cop.

“I should stab this bitch right now.” Pauleena thought as she and Remy entered the staircase and headed downstairs towards the mess hall along with all the other inmates.

When Pauleena and Remy reached the second floor landing they spotted Tina and about twelve Spades standing around looking like they were up to no good. Immediately Pauleena knew that Tina and The Spades were lingering around in the staircase waiting around for her to show up.

When Tina spotted Pauleena she quickly removed a shank from the small of her back as her and The Spades began making their way up the stairs while Pauleena and Remy were coming down.

When Remy spotted The Spades she stopped mid-stride and froze right where she stood. She didn't know if she should run or stay and fight. "What's the play?" Remy asked with a nervous and scared look on her face.

"We ain't running" Pauleena said as she discreetly removed her shank from her pocket. When Tina and The Spades got close enough, Pauleena shoved her shank deep in the middle of Remy's back. Remy's eyes lit up with pain and shock as she turned around and looked at Pauleena, all while trying to touch the entry wound in her back.

"Snitches get stitches!" Pauleena growled as she plunged the shank deep inside Remy's stomach, then broke the handle off so Remy wouldn't be able to remove the blade. "Fuck the police!" She yelled then shoved Remy back into the arms of The Spades.

Tina and The Spades took turns stabbing Remy like she was an animal, then tossed her body down the remaining stairs like she was a piece of trash. Tina went to stab Pauleena next, but it was too late Pauleena had already took off running back up the stairs.

"You can't run forever bitch!" Tina yelled before her and The Spades quickly left the scene of the crime.

When Pauleena made it back upstairs she ran straight to the police bubble. She hated the police, but there was no way she could stay in the prison another day. The Spades were too deep in the prison system and there was nowhere for Pauleena to run or hide. Pauleena had no other choice but to tell the C.O. that she felt like her life was in danger, so she should get transferred to another prison and away from The Spades. Even though it would probably be Spades in any jail, she went to;

Pauleena knew all she had to do was survive for only a few more days until her release date.

“Fuck it; I gotta what I gotta do.” Pauleena said to herself as she walked up to the C.O.’s station.

Chapter Nineteen

Fight Night

The Terminator sat in his dressing room getting his hands wrapped as several camera crews filmed and recorded his every move. Usually The Terminator's dressing room was full of life and excitement, but this time was different everyone in the dressing room all were serious no nonsense looks on their faces.

Lisa sat over in the corner with a scared and nervous look on her face. She didn't know what to expect or how the outcome of the fight would turn out, she just didn't want to see her man get hurt. Over the last couple of month's Lisa found herself falling madly in love with the arrogant boxer.

Sitting on the other side of the dressing room sat Snow; he flew all the way out to Russia to support his friend and to celebrate The Terminator's victory once the fight was over. Snow cut his eyes at Lisa he still didn't like her nor had he forgotten that she was there when Live Wire had *snuck* him in the restaurant. But Snow decided to keep his thoughts and comments to himself out of respect for The Terminator.

As The Terminator sat getting his hands wrapped, a dark skin chick with a fat ass stood behind him massaging his shoulders and rubbing oil over his body, as she massaged him and rubbed oil over his body she whispered in his ear over and over again. "You're the greatest boxer ever."

Over on the sideline Lisa found herself jealous that another woman had her hands all over her man, but this same woman had been working with The Terminator for years so there wasn't too much she could say about it, but as she watched the woman whisper in her man's ear she couldn't help but wonder if The Terminator had slept with or was sleeping with the woman or not.

"You ready to do this?" Mr. Wilson asked while The Terminator got his gloves laced up. For the past four weeks Mr. Wilson had The Terminator sparring with fighters in higher weight classes to get him prepared for what was to come tonight and Mr. Wilson had to admit that his fighter looked great. After watching tape after tape on Brutus, Mr. Wilson realized that The Terminator was indeed going to be the best fighter that Brutus ever faced and honestly Mr. Wilson liked their chances.

"I was born ready." The Terminator replied. The sound of eighty thousand Russian fight fans singing their national anthem invaded his dressing room walls. The Terminator knew that eighty thousand riled up, drunk fight fans cheering against him was going to be a challenge in itself, but The Terminator was up for the challenge. The leather boxing gloves on his hands were forest green, his leather boxing trunks were also forest green and down on The Terminator's feet were a pair of custom made forest green high top Prada boxing shoes.

The Terminator began to shadow box to keep himself loose until it was time for him to be escorted out to the ring. In the back of The Terminator's mind he knew millions of dollars was riding on this fight, fight fans had bet their homes and their life savings on the outcome of the fight.

"It's your world." Snow said giving The Terminator a fist bump. "Now let's get this money." Snow had $50,000 riding on the fight and couldn't wait to collect.

Seconds later a loud knock could be heard at the door. One of The Terminator's body guards answered the door, said a few words shut the door, then turned and faced The Terminator and said, “It’s time to go.”

The Terminator gave Lisa a kiss. “I love you.”

“I love you too baby.” Lisa said with a worried and scared look on her face. “Good luck.” She said as she was then escorted to her front row seat by one of the promoters.

The dark skin chick who had oiled up The Terminator’s body slipped a custom made forest green mink with the sleeves cut off around the champ’s arms and flipped the deep hood over his head.

The Terminator and his team said a quick prayer, then were out the door. The Terminator, his entourage and team of security spilled out into the hallway. Two camera men walked backwards, not wanting to miss a move that The Terminator made. As The Terminator walked down the hall the noise from all of the fight fans cheering and screaming had the floor vibrating under his feet, he could feel the electricity in the air, tonight was going to be a historic fight as well as an historic night.

The Terminator and his crew stood at the entrance waiting to be told when they could head to the ring, when Mr. Wilson placed his lips close to his fighters ear so he could hear him over the loud crowd. “This is it, ain’t no turning back!” He yelled. “This motherfucker said he was gon knock you the fuck out in front of the whole world, you gon sit back and let this motherfucker knock you out? Huh?” Mr. Wilson yelled. “You lose this fight; no more big money fights for you, without no money ain’t no more fancy cars, big jewelry and last but not least no more hoes! You gon let this motherfucker take your hoes?” Mr. Wilson continued to try and motivate his fighter. “This Russian motherfucker wants to be you, you gon let this motherfucker take your spot!? Huh!?” He yelled. “You go out there and show all these motherfuckers why you the greatest fighter in the world.”

The sound of Jay-Z song "I show you how to do this." Blasting through the speakers informed The Terminator that it was time to head down to the ring.

The Terminator began to slowly make his way towards the ring. When the Russian crowd spotted him they immediately began to boo him. The Terminator ignored the loud chant of Boo's and continued towards the ring. The Terminator's body guards had to slap several of the Russian fight fans hands away as the fans tried to kill themselves just to get a touch of the champ. The walk down to the ring was a bumpy one, but after a whole lot of pushing and shoving, The Terminator finally entered the ring.

"Stick to the game plan and this will be an easy fight; whatever you do don't try to exchange with this guy." Mr. Wilson told him. "You are the better fighter, the smarter fighter and the more skilled fighter…do what you do….this is going to be….."

Suddenly everything went completely black, every light in the arena went out, and seconds later the light from the big screen that hung from the middle of the ceiling illuminated the arena as the video of Brutus knocking out a horse replayed over and over again causing the crowd to go into a frenzy.

The lights slowly came back on as the sound of some unusual Russian music blasted though the speakers, announcing that Brutus was about to make his entrance to the ring.

Minutes later the crowd began to cheer as Brutus was escorted to the ring draped in all red, representing the color of his country. Several fight fans waved the Russian flag back and forth through the air, as Brutus the Russian sensation made his way inside the ring.

When Brutus removed his red robe, his body looked as if someone had drew it and placed it on his body, his body looked so muscular that it looked like it was deformed.

"Both fighters in the middle of the ring!" The referee announced, he along with millions of fight fans were ready for the action to get underway.

The Terminator and Brutus met face to face in the middle of the ring while the referee went over the rules.

"I want clean fight gentlemen, I went over rules with both of you in the back, keep the punches above the belt and when I say break, I expect y'all to break....touch gloves and let's have a good fight." The referee said in a stern tone.

"Let's make this an easy night." Mr. Wilson said slipping a clear mouth piece in The Terminator's mouth. "Just like we do it in the gym, one round at a time." He kissed The Terminator on the cheek before slipping out the ring.

The Terminator looked out into the front row and spotted Lisa sitting there with a look of worry on her face; he winked at her, then turned his attention on his opponent. Brutus stood at the other end of the ring bouncing up and down, slapping his gloves together extra hard giving him the dirtiest look ever.

The Terminator flashed a smile and blew his opponent a kiss in an attempt to piss him off even further.

Ding! Ding! Ding!

At sound of the bell fight fans stood to their feet and began cheering loudly in anticipation of a great fight.

The Terminator slowly walked to the center of the ring, while Brutus trotted. They met at the center. The Terminator stuck his glove out waiting for Brutus to tap it with his own glove a move most fighters did out of respect, Brutus ignored the gesture and lunged toward The Terminator throwing a powerful sweeping right hook. The Terminator managed to just barely weave the hook just before it got a chance to connect. The Terminator flashed a smile, then landed a jab in the center of Brutus' face forcing his head to snap back. The Terminator danced around gracefully, while Brutus flat footedly did his best to cut the ring off. When Brutus came within striking distance The Terminator threw another jab that landed in the center of Brutus' forehead, Brutus tried to move his head in time, but The Terminator's hand speed was much faster than he anticipated. The Terminator then faked another jab, but instead leaped and landed a check-hook to the side of Brutus's face, then followed up with a right cross that landed square on Brutus' chin causing his head to snap to the right.

"That's right stick and move!" Mr. Wilson yelled from the corner.

From the look on Brutus face, The Terminator could tell that the punches he was landing weren't hurting him, but they were definitely beginning to piss him off.

The Terminator threw another quick jab, then tried to slide to his right side to get out of Brutus' reach, but Brutus beat him to the step and cornered him near the ropes. Immediately The Terminator got into his Philly shell defensive stance, the same defensive style that Floyd Mayweather Jr. was famous for and prepared to slip Brutus onslaught of punches.

Brutus fired off a powerful left hook followed by a right hook. The first punch The Terminator blocked with his glove, while the other punch bounced off his shoulder, Brutus went to throw another punch, but The Terminator landed a quick counter right uppercut, that lifted his head up, then was gone before Brutus's next punch even had a chance of landing.

The Terminator faked high, then went low and landed a stiff jab in the pit of Brutus's stomach just as the bell rang.

Ding! Ding! Ding!

Both fighters quickly headed back to their corners.

"What I told you?" Mr. Wilson said excitedly as he extended the water bottle and squirted a mouthful of water in The Terminator's mouth. "This motherfucker can't fight, he just hit hard."

The Terminator swished the water around in his mouth before spitting it into a bucket. "He can't handle my speed and accuracy."

"Stick to the plan and this will be an easy fight." Mr. Wilson said as the bell sounded off announcing the beginning of round two. Again The Terminator and Brutus met in the center of the ring and The Terminator picked up right where he left off and landed a jab, followed by a quick right cross. Before Brutus could even think about throwing a punch or combination of his own, The Terminator was gone. Brutus had to admit the The Terminator's foot work was outstanding as well as his boxing skills, but Brutus had a trick for all that. He took two more jabs to the face, then cut the ring off again and just like he suspected The Terminator slipped into his Philly Shell defensive stance. Brutus took both of his gloves and jammed them into The Terminator's chest pushing him back against the ropes. The move had left The Terminator off balance and before he had a chance to recover, Brutus was all up in his grill. Brutus threw a powerful hook that landed on side of The Terminator's face causing his head to violently snap to the side, he followed up with a digging right hook to the body.

"Ughh!" The Terminator grunted as he felt Brutus's power. It felt as if the man was fighting with loaded gloves, the hook that Brutus landed had The Terminator's ear ringing. He tried to dance his way off the ropes, but Brutus shoved him back against the ropes and fired off a lightening quick four punch combination. The Terminator tried to block the onslaught of punches, but three out of four of the punches managed to slip through his guard and land flush on his chin. Before Brutus could land another punch, The Terminator quickly grabbed a hold of Brutus arms, a wise veteran move, this move gave him a chance to clear his head, regroup and get his thoughts together.

"That's all you got?" The Terminator said in Brutus ear. When the referee separated. The two, The Terminator landed a straight right hand lead that snapped Brutus' head back just as the bell rang.

Ding! Ding! Ding!

When The Terminator reached the corner Mr. Wilson was already in his ass, before he even got a chance to sit down.

"Stay off the ropes!" He yelled in The Terminators face. "Don't fight his fight! Stick to the game plan son."

Ding! Ding! Ding!

The third round started off with The Terminator landing his jab at will. Every time Brutus tried to close the distance between the two, The Terminator landed a swift, stiff jab. "Get back!" The Terminator danced away as blood began to stream from Brutus' nose.

The Terminator backed up into the corner trying to lure Brutus in and make him think that he was trapped off. Brutus took the bait and The Terminator landed a powerful sweeping right hook. Brutus head brutally snapped top the right as sweat went flying from his face. He somehow managed to walk right through the powerful punch and land a hook of his own, The Terminator answered back with a left and right hook. From there the two traded a few more power punches as the crowd went wild.

Ding! Ding! Ding!

"Don't exchange with him." Mr. Wilson yelled as he cleaned the cut on The Terminator's left eye. "And stay away from his right hand."

The next three rounds were identical to the third round. The Terminator allowed his pride to get in the way and found himself in the ring mixing it up with Brutus and the end result was him taking unnecessary punishment. The fight could of been so easy, but The Terminator wanted to prove to the world that his chin wasn't made out of glass and he could in fact take a punch.

The bell sounded announcing the beginning of round seven. The Terminator started the round off again landing his jab at will. "Get back stupid!" He taunted. "I said get back!" He said landing another jab on the bridge of Brutus' nose. Brutus threw a jab of his own, but The Terminator side stepped the jab and countered with a check hook to Brutus' chin followed by a right hook to the mid-section, before Brutus got a chance to throw another punch, The Terminator quickly tied him up by grabbing his arms. "And I'm still going to fuck your wife." He said in Brutus' ear as the referee separated the two.

The Terminator danced an arrogant dance as he began to pull away with the fight. His defense, foot work and boxing skill were too much for the Russian champ. The Terminator weaved another one of Brutus' punches and landed an uppercut followed by a right cross that caused the crowd to "eeeewwww and aaahhhhh!"

"Horses don't hit back." The Terminator taunted as another jab landed in the center of Brutus' face.

Frustrated because he wasn't able to land a clean solid blow, Brutus faked high and went low and landed a powerful shot below The Terminator's cup.

"Ughhh!" The Terminator growled as he dropped down to his knees, then rolled over onto his back. His eyes shut tight and the look of severe pain was etched across his face.

Instead of stopping the action for a moment due to the low blow, the referee began counting; he was calling the low blow a knock down.

"One...two....three...four...five...six...seven."

On the count of seven The Terminator some how managed to crawl back up to his feet, he was in severe pain, but his pride refused to let him go out like that.

Brutus quickly closed the distance between the two and threw a powerful punch, The Terminator weaved and avoided getting punched directly in his face, but his chin took the brunt of the blow. His legs got tangled, throwing him off balance for a second. The Terminator instantly raised his gloves and managed to protect his face from the onslaught, but every time Brutus's fist connected with his forearms he could feel his bones rattle from the powerful punches.

Ding! Ding! Ding!

Back in the corner Mr. Wilson rung a wet sponge out over top of The Terminator's head.

"They cheating," The Terminator winced still affected by the low blow. "I knew they were going to try and do some cheating bullshit, I knew it."

"Don't sweat that shit." Mr. Wilson yelled sticking a glob of Vaseline in the open cut above his fighter's eye. "You built for this shit, just keep on doing what you doing and stay off the ropes."

"These judges are going to try and rob me." The Terminator spat.

"Well don't give them crackers the chance to rob you, you got five rounds left to knock this Russian piece of shit out!" Mr. Wilson yelled.

Ding! Ding! Ding!

Brutus and The Terminator met in the center of the ring and Brutus got things started, he fired off a four punch combination that The Terminator blocked rather easily, he then answered back with a leaping left hook that caused sweat and blood to fly from Brutus' face. Brutus had his guards up. But the hook was so quick that it still landed flush on his chin.

The Terminator flashed a smile as his glove bounced off of Brutus's face again. Finally Brutus got desperate and lunged forward and threw a wild hook; The Terminator easily weaved the hook and countered with a devastating upper cut that stunned Brutus. His legs got tangled up as he did a drunken dance that caused the crowd to cheer in excitement, in anticipation of a knock out.

Brutus desperately tried to reach out and grab and hold The Terminator in an attempt to keep from getting hit again and regroup, but The Terminator had other plans. The Terminator took a step back and landed another uppercut to Brutus's chin followed by a hook to the temple.

"Get ya hands off me you bitch ass nigga!" The Terminator growled. He had Brutus' right where he wanted him and wasn't about to let him off the hook. He quickly closed the distance between the two and went to work; he fired off a left-right-left-right-right-right-left combination and finished it off with a left and right hook that put Brutus down on the canvas. When The Terminator saw Brutus hit the floor and his mouth piece slide out of his mouth he knew that the battle was finally over.

The referee did a slow drag out count until he finally reached ten and the bell sounded.

Ding! Ding! Ding!

Reporters, boxing analyst and camera men flooded the ring, while The Terminator climbed to the top of the ropes in the corner and raised his gloves up in the air as he gladly accepted the boo's that came from the crowd.

"You did it!" Mr. Wilson yelled with a huge smile on his face as he gave The Terminator a big bear hug and rocked back and forth. After all the hard work in the gym it was well worth it.

"These motherfuckers can't fuck with me." The Terminator boasted as a boxing analyst strolled up on him and began to do a post fight intervention.

"Great fight tonight." the analyst began. "What was going through your mind in the mid-rounds?"

"The only thing going through my mind was how pretty I am." The Terminator flashed an arrogant smile.

"Tell me about the low blow."

"It was a cheap shot, but when you're fighting a low life that's to be expected." The Terminator shrugged, "It is what it is, I came into Brutus's backyard and kicked his ass....shit wasn't bout nothing."

"Who do you plan on fighting next?" The analyst asked.

"I'm going to take a vacation, spend some time with my family; I'm not even sure if I even want to fight anymore. I've made enough money in this sport and I think I'm done."

"So are you telling the world that this was the last time seeing The Terminator in action?" The analyst held the microphone up to The Terminator's mouth.

"I am officially retired." The Terminator smiled for the cameras, then left. He had given the boxing world seventeen years of his life and now it was time for him to sit back and enjoy his *hard* earned money. When The Terminator reached his dressing room, Lisa ran and jumped into his arms.

"Congratulations baby!" She squealed, "You did it!"

"I'm done with this boxing shit!" The Terminator huffed as he walked over and took a seat over on the leather sofa. "I'm done." He said as tears began to stream down his cheeks. "Thanks for everything you've done for me in my career." He sobbed looking up at Mr. Wilson.

"My pleasure." Mr. Wilson smiled. "Whatever decision you make I'm behind you a hundred percent."

Before The Terminator could say another word, the dark skin chick with the fat ass slid behind him and began to massage his shoulders affectionately.

"I mean damn!" Lisa huffed as she stared at the dark skin chick with fire dancing in her eyes. "Can I massage my own man's shoulders?"

"Calm down baby." The Terminator told her.

"Nah, calm down my ass. I'm tired of this bitch always sniffing around my man." Lisa continued to rant and rave. "The fight is over with, what is this bitch still doing here?"

The Terminator nodded towards his security and instantly the six foot nine monster escorted Lisa out of the dressing room.

Right now The Terminator wasn't in the mood for no foolishness; all he wanted to do was enjoy the victory.

"I thought that bitch would never leave." Snow said drawing laughter from everyone in the dressing room. "Fuck that bullshit it's time to celebrate." He said pulling a bottle of champagne from out of a book bag. "Let's see what these Russian bitches is about."

Chapter Twenty

Home Sweet Home

Pauleena stepped foot out of the prison's gate and took a deep sniff of the fresh air. Finally she was a free woman again and couldn't wait to get back into the swing of things. It felt good to be away from all the grimy, bum ass bitches and back out into the *real* world. Pauleena stepped out of the Prison draped in a snow white mink, a pair of oversized white designer shades covered her eyes and she wore her hair in neat cornrows going straight back that stopped near her lower back. A white spandex fitting skirt made by Michael Kors hugged her curvy frame; her legs had a fresh coat of baby oil on them and glistened with each step she took. On her feet were a pair of expensive white open toe sling backs with a nice heel, her toes were plain with no polish, but still pretty.

Pauleena strutted with a confident run way type of work, a huge smile spread across her lips when she spotted Psycho leaning up against the hood of the cocaine white stretch hummer with a bottle of expensive champagne in his hand.

"There's my superstar." Psycho smiled with open arms. He had dreamt of this day so many nights and finally it had arrived.

"Oooooh my god!" Pauleena squealed, melting into Psycho's arms. "I've missed you like crazy!" She stood up on her tippy toes and gave psycho a slow, long, wet drawn out tongue kiss. Psycho opened the door to the hummer, scooped Pauleena up into his arms and slid in the back of the Hummer. As soon as the back door closed shut the driver of the Hummer quickly pulled out into the street and away from the prison.

Pauleena kicked off her heels and held out a wine glass. Psycho quickly filled it with champagne. Pauleena raised the glass up to her mouth and killed the champagne in one shot." You missed me?"

"Like crazy," Psycho replied. Ever since Pauleena had been released he couldn't keep from smiling like a kid in a candy store.

"What about him?" Pauleena nodded towards Psycho's crotch. "He missed me?"

Psycho flashed a devilish grin as he undid his pants and pulled out his dick and began to slowly stroke it in his hand. "Why don't you come ask him yourself?" He challenged.

Pauleena's mouth began to water at the sight of Psycho's dick. It had been so long since she had seen one that the sight of it set her body on fire.

Pauleena grabbed Psycho and roughly tossed him down to the floor of the Hummer.

Psycho smiled, "Damn baby that's what the fuck I'm talking....."

"Don't you say another word!" Pauleena hushed him. She stood right over Psycho's face, hiked her skirt up and squatted down on his face. "Eat this pussy and don't you dare say another word!" she demanded.

Psycho lay on his back and stared up at Pauleena's hairy pussy, she usually kept it waxed, but due to her circumstances she was little on the furry side.

"Oh shit." Pauleena purred loudly. "That's right Daddy, that's right Daddy....eee, eeew, ahhhh" She moaned as she pressed her weight down on his mouth. Her skirt covered Psycho's head as she grinded against his nose, his chin, she moved on the hardness of his chin, giving his face a nice slow ride. "I'm about to cum all over your face!" She announced. The loud wet slurping sounds that were rising beneath her turned her on even more. Pauleena rode Psycho's face like she was possessed, she moved like she was no longer in charge of her body.

"Ahh, yes, yes, ahhh!" Her orgasm came hard and fast and in a series of waves, but Psycho wasn't done yet. He was just getting started. He flicked his tongue like a lizard, accepted all of Pauleena's wetness and gave Pauleena's pussy lips a nice slow tongue kiss. A tongue kiss that Pauleena thought would never end. She moaned, panted, made noises as if she was being tortured with each lick that was delivered to her love box. Psycho sucked on Pauleena's clit, then began to slightly nibble on it. That move caused Pauleena to cream all over his face and mouth area again.

While riding Psycho's face, Pauleena heard a few moans escape from his lips, heard sounds like he was trying to speak or say something, but her fat, wet juicy pussy muffles his words. "Yes, yes, right there! Right there!" Pauleena threw her head back with her eyes shut tight and her mouth in an "O". Pauleena moved until everything became urgent, labored breath thickened as sweat rose, she jerked and moaned, jerked and moaned until a powerful orgasm took control over her body.

Psycho, then guided Pauleena, made her straddle him, eased his way inside, then guided Pauleena, eased his way inside of her insides. He watched as her face crumbled up as he slowly entered her tight walls.

"Ahhh!" Pauleena moaned in a voice just above a whisper. It had been so long since something had been inserted in her that she had to get readjusted to Psycho's size. She slowly began to bounce up and down at a nice slow rhythm, her hips moving like a Latino dancer. "This is all your pussy!" She moaned in a sexy porn star type of voice.

Psycho pulled Pauleena's long braided hair as she rode him, looked at her as she moved, stared into her haunting eyes, "You missed this dick!?"

"Yes, I missed this dick so much!" Pauleena moaned.

"I can't hear you!" Psycho growled through clenched teeth as he gave Pauleena's ass a hard slap.

Smack!

"Oh yes Daddy. I missed this dick; oh I missed this dick so much!"

"I can't hear you!"

Smack!

"Oh my god, I'm about to cum again."

Pauleena moved up and down, going up easy coming down hard, did that over and over. Psycho held on to Pauleena's petite waist made her his prisoner, let her move, let her roll and gyrate, let her move up and down, her moans loud, serve, and never ending.

Psycho cupped Pauleena ass and spread both of her cheek open as he began to thrust upward, he went in and out of her so fast, so deep, keeping his stroke long and steady. "Ride this dick!" He yelled as he began to pump even harder. Pauleena screamed like each stroke was killing her, screamed like she had waited three and half years to get fucked like this, she sank her nails down in Psycho's flesh and bounced her ass up and down at a super fast pace, the sound of Pauleena's skin slapping against Psycho's skin sounded off loudly sounding like the ultimate battle.

"No, you gon ride this dick today! You gon ride this dick!" Psycho yelled. "Ya Daddy about to cum! Ride this dick, ride it!"

"Ahh, ahh, ahh yes Daddy cum in this wet pussy!" Pauleena screamed as she began riding the dick even faster, she closed her eyes, her breathing intense, her body trembling, panting, her and Psycho both let out animalistic sounds as they reached their orgasms at the same time.

When Pauleena was done moaning she stayed on top of Psycho and caught her breath. "You are an animal." She huffed bending down to kiss Psycho's lips; she could taste her pussy still fresh on his breath.

"I'm your animal." Psycho smiled as he got up and refilled him and Pauleena's wine glasses with champagne.

"Now let's get back to business." Pauleena sat cross legged and took a slow sip of her drink. "What's up with The Big Show and The Spades?"

"Since The Spades have joined forces with us our numbers have been sky rocketing through the roof." Psycho told her "With them having so many members on the payroll it makes it easier for us to expand and take over more territory, not to mention we're recruiting more and more members to the team each day." He pointed out.

"Can we trust him?" Pauleena asked taking another sip from her drink. The only thing that worried her was The Big Show thinking that since he had all the muscle that he no longer needed her services anymore and tried to over throw her like he had done to Dice.

"So far his word has been gold." Psycho said. "But just to be on the safe side I got Prince and Tall Man keeping a close eye on The Big Show."

"Set up a meeting with this clown."

"When?"

"Today," Pauleena spat. "I need to look in his eyes and see what's what."

"Say no more I got you."

"Still no sign of Wolf?" Pauleena asked. Her stay in prison had been a rough one and it was all because of Wolf. Pauleena had been away on vacation minding her own business when she got a call telling her that a man named Wolf and The Spades had been interfering with her money and ever since he'd been a problem. Pauleena and Wolf had a never ending beef and if the two ever bumped into each other again, someone was more than likely to lose their life on site.

"Nah, that pussy has been M.I.A. now since you went away." Psycho told her. "He probably knows if he ever steps feet back in New York again he's going to get his head blown off."

The strength Hummer pulled up in front of Pauleena's mansion. "What's up?" Psycho smiled, "Round two?"

Pauleena couldn't help but smile, "We'll save that for later, go bring The Big Show back to me and we can play later." She said, then slid out the back of the Hummer. Immediately Pauleena was met by a team of Muslim security.

"I love you baby. I'll see you in a few." Psycho said out the back window as the Hummer pulled off.

When Pauleena stepped foot in her mansion all she could do was smile. "I'm back." she said in a voice just above a whisper. She removed her white mink and handed it to her head Muslim body guard and enforcer a monster in a suit and a boe-tie that went by the name "Big Ock."

"I'm going to go take a shower. I don't want to be disturbed" Pauleena said over her shoulder as she walked up the stairs carrying her heels in her hand. Once in her bedroom Pauleena stripped down butt naked and prepared to hop in the hot tub.

Pauleena relaxed in the hot tub and let the jets massage her body. The feeling seemed a little unreal at first. Pauleena sipped on a strong drink and just enjoyed the sound of the jets humming. She wiggled her toes and frowned at the way they looked, she couldn't remember the last time her toes went without being done and polished and the sight alone disgusted her. *"I gotta get back on my shit."* Pauleena said to herself as she hopped out the tub, dried off and walked around the house butt naked something she had been dying to do for the last few years. Pauleena walked over and opened up her gun closet and just stared at her collection for a couple of minutes while she took out her braids. The sight of all the guns staring back at her gave her a rush. As she sat there looking in the gun closet, she envisioned herself blowing Wolf's head off with the crome desert eagle that was calling her name.

A light knock on the door pulled Pauleena from her thoughts. "Yo." she called out.

"You have a guest here to see you." Big Ock announced.

"What the fuck!" Pauleena barked, "Didn't I say I didn't want to be disturbed? Whoever is here tell em I don't want to be seen today." She spat. Immediately Pauleena figured the guest that popped up at her home was Mr. Goldberg coming to harass her for more money, Pauleena threw on a pair of white linen pants and a white wife beater when she heard another knock at her bedroom door. Pauleena walked and snatched her bedroom door open. "Wassup now?"

"This guest refuses to leave." Big Ock said, "I was getting ready to put hands and feet on em, but they *insist* that they speak to you."

Pauleena sighed loudly as she brushed past her head security guard, and headed downstairs towards the door. Whoever was knocking on her door better of had a good reason for it, or else it was sure to be some problems.

Pauleena opened the door and found an attractive woman standing on the other side holding a dozen roses. Pauleena tried to recognize the face of the woman that stood before her, but her mind drew a black. "May I help you?"

"Yes, I'm here to see Psycho."

"And may I ask who you are?"

"My name is Monica; do you know what time Psycho will be back in?" She asked innocently.

"Why the fuck you coming to my home asking about my fiancé?" Pauleena asked; she was seconds away from punching the woman in her mouth.

"Oh, you're Pauleena?" Monica asked as if she was shocked and didn't know who she was. "Listen I think we need to talk. May I come in?"

Pauleena thought on it for a second, then stepped to the side allowing Monica to enter the mansion. Pauleena led Monica to a table and the two women had a seat.

"Okay I'm listening." Pauleena said with a serious look on her face.

"Listen Pauleena," Monica began, "I'mma keep it tall with you, me and Psycho are in love and we were thinking about getting married, but Psycho didn't want to *dump* you while you were in jail, I'm not tryna step on ya toes or nothing ma, but that's my man and I'm riding with him"

"You fucked Psycho?" Pauleena asked; she just wanted to be clear on what she was hearing.

"No." Monica said, "Me and Psycho don't fuck, we *make love*." she said making it sound way worse than it actually was.

"So what are you here for?"

"Me and Psycho would like to move on with our lives and he doesn't want you making any trouble for us." Monica smirked.

"Word? how long you been messing around with Psycho for?" Pauleena asked trying to hide the hurt in her face.

"Since you been in jail." Monica told her. "I just wanted to come over here and have a woman to woman talk with you, and to be honest I don't really feel comfortable with you being around my man and all that, sooooo before things get out of hand and go left, I'm asking that you please stay the fuck away from *my man*." she said in a tough guy tone of voice.

"Or else what?" Pauleena challenged, "What you gon do?"

Monica sensed the tension building and wasn't about to back down, Psycho was her man and she didn't have a problem fighting to prove her love. "Look" Monica said, "Don't come at me with that jail shit, Psycho doesn't want to be with you anymore, he wants to be with me and you ain't got no choice but to respect it."

"I respect it." Pauleena conceded. She wasn't even mad; she was more hurt by Psycho's disloyalty and infidelity than anything else. The chick sitting in front of her talking tough didn't concern or worry her one bit; she was more focused on what she was going to do to Psycho. He violated by having another woman show up to their home and that alone was what pissed Pauleena off the most.

"You better cause I don't play when it comes to my man!" Monica snapped. She looked Pauleena up and down and frowned when she got to Pauleena's feet.

"What?" Pauleena asked picking up on the funny look on Monica's face.

"Nothing, I just thought you would be, you know." She paused, "A lil more prettier and have a lil more swag, I mean ain't you a millionaire?" she chuckled.

"I see." Pauleena nodded her head up and down as her eyes made contact with the roses Monica held in her hands. "These roses are they for Psycho?"

"Pretty ain't they?" Monica hissed.

"Here, let me take these and put them in some water." Pauleena said reaching for the dozen roses.

"Be careful with these, I spent some change on them." Monica said handing Pauleena the roses. Pauleena took the roses, put them up to her nose and inhaled deeply. Without warning Pauleena spun and slapped Monica across the face with the roses, sending pretty red rose petals flying all over the place. She grabbed Monica by the back of her head, by her weave and slammed her face down into the oak wood table a couple times. The sound of Monica's face bouncing off the table sounded off loudly, before she slithered down to the floor.

"Bitch you wanna come to my house and start talking crazy!" Pauleena growled as she raised her bare feet and stomped Monica's face down into the floor. "You fucking my man....then wanna come over here and talk all that fly shit. Bitch don't ya ever in yo life disrespect the Queen like you ain't got no fucking sense!"

All the ruckus caused Big Ock and a few other of Pauleena's Muslim body guards to storm around the corner to see what all the commotion was about.

"You aight boss?" Big Ock asked looking down at a bloody half conscious Monica that lay before Pauleena' s feet, then smiled.

"Nah, I ain't alright." Pauleena huffed. "Gimme the hawk" (knife)

Big Ock gladly passed Pauleena a flip out knife. "Handle your business."

Once Pauleena had the knife in her hand she went to work on Monica. She cut and stabbed Monica each and every way until the woman that lay before her was no more. "Trifling ass bitch!" She growled as she looked down and noticed that her white outfit was covered in blood. "Bitch made me ruin my outfit."

"Welcome home." Big Ock smiled as he watched two Muslim guards drag Monica away by her ankles.

Pauleena glanced at the surveillance cameras and saw the stretch Hummer pull up, followed by an all black van. She walked up to Big Ock and removed his P89 from his holster."Tell the boys to come straight to my office." She said and walked off.

Big Ock smirked as he watched Pauleena's hips and ass switch from side to side with each step she took. He was liking his new position already and could tell that he was going to enjoy working with his new boss.

Minutes later Psycho, Prince, Tall Man and The Big Show and a few Spades entered the foyer, laughing and joking.

"Pauleena wants to see all of youz immediately." Big Ock told the group, then led them upstairs to Pauleena's office. All of the laughing and joking stopped instantly when they entered the office and spotted Pauleena sitting at her desk with her feet kicked up, with blood covering her clothes and a gun in her hand.

"Baby what happened?" Psycho asked in a lovingly concerned tone. "Are you alright?"

Pauleena stood to her feet, snatched the bottle of Absolute of the desk and took a big swig straight out of the bottle, then focused on Psycho. "Your *girlfriend* Monica came to see me today and we had a *long talk*." She said letting the gun dangle by her side. "She had some interesting things to tell me."

"I can explain." Psycho said defensively.

"Explain what?" Pauleena barked. "How you were fucking her brains out? Huh? Is that what you gon explain?"

"Baby it's not even like that." Psycho tried to explain, but a bullet to his thigh hushed him and sent him crumbling down to the floor.

Boc!

The sound of the gun discharging caused everyone in the office to jump, no one was expecting for Pauleena to actually shoot Psycho.

"You violated!" Pauleena walked up and stood over Psycho.

"Baby, I'm sorry." Psycho pleaded.

Pauleena fired another shot into Psycho's other leg. "No, I'm sorry. I'm sorry that I trusted you and gave you a second chance."

"I love you baby, don't do this."

"I love you too." Pauleena whispered, then fired a shot that landed right between Psycho's eyes, turning the floor in the office into a bloody mess.

Pauleena slowly walked over and sat back behind her desk. In a quick motion she slung the bottle of absolute that she held in her hand at the wall and watched it explode in a spray of glass. "Get out!" She said in a voice just above a whisper as tears began to rain down her face. Pauleena loved Psycho with all of her heart, but t his was the second time that he had broken her heart, and abused her trust. She knew if she let him get away with it a second time, then more than likely it would be a third time and so on and so on. "I said get the fuck out!" She yelled when nobody moved, it was as if everyone was in shock.

Two Muslim bodyguards drug Psycho out of Pauleena's office by his ankles, leaving a dark red nasty trail of blood behind.

The Big Show slowly walked up to Pauleena's desk. "Sorry we had to meet on such bad circumstances, but I brought you a coming home present." He said laying a folded piece of paper down on Pauleena's desk, the then turned and followed Prince's lead out of the office.

Pauleena sat at her desk and cried her eyes out for the next two hours. She couldn't believe that after doing time that she would have to come home and kill the man that she loved. She was supposed to come home and get married, maybe have a kid or two, enjoy some of her money, not have Monica show up to her door to inform her of Psycho's infidelity. After crying her eyes out, Pauleena finally picked up the folded piece of paper and glanced down at it. In the folded piece of paper was Wolf's address. Pauleena didn't know how The Big Show had managed to stumble across Wolf's out of town address, but she was thankful for the information and definitely planned on putting it to use....sooner than later.

Chapter Twenty One

Make Up Sex

"I love you." Live Wire said staring across the table in the Japanese restaurant at Sparkle. After what had went down at the lounge with Tori or The Madam as everyone else called her, Live Wire called himself making it up to Sparkle. Yeah he may have had a lot of women, but Sparkle was his main joint and the only chick he had ever loved and tonight he had a special night planned to show Sparkle just how much she meant to him.

"I love you too." Sparkle said cheesing from ear to ear. She had on a leopard print one piece cat suit that clung to her body like a second skin. Sparkle noticed that every few seconds Live Wire kept on glancing around, she also noticed that several Real Spades scattered around the restaurant. "You alright?"

"Yeah, I'm good. That Agent Starks shit just got me all paranoid." He said. For men of the law to just open fire on site without an explanation bothered Live Wire and was beginning to fuck with his mind. Before Live Wire got a chance to say another word a man wearing a Yankee fitted and a drunk look in his eyes walked up to their table.

"Ooooooh shit my bad." The drunken man said loudly. "I thought you was *Nicki*, I was looking over here to see if I could get an autograph." He said looking down at Sparkle.

"No, sorry I'm *not* Nicki Manaj." Sparkle said flashing a friendly smile.

"Sorry to had disturbed y'all." The drunken man said looking down at Live Wire.

"Yo step off!" Live Wire said in a dismissive manner. He was hoping that the drunk fool gave him a reason to put hands and feet on him, but instead the drunk man left quietly.

Sparkle looked over and saw that Live Wire had a sour look on his face. "I know you ain't in ya feelings over that Bozo, who just walked up to our table."

"What are you talking about?" Live Wire asked faking innocence.

"Nigga please." Sparkle spat, "With all the bitches you keep in ya face and all the cheating you do, I should be able to get away with a compliment. Shit I let you get away with murder!"

"Aight, it's time to go." Live Wire stood up from the booth and exited the restaurant not caring if Sparkle was behind him or not. He was tired of going back and forth with her over the smallest of things. When Live Wire stepped foot outside the restaurant he spotted a light skin chick with a long nice blonde weave standing there with her arms folded across her chest. Next to her stood an older man whose body looked kind of frail, he wore faded blue jeans, a t-shirt and some run down sneakers.

"Oh, so you can't speak?" The chick said with an attitude. By now Sparkle had exited the restaurant with a mean scowl on her face.

"I'm sorry, do I know you?" Live Wire faked like he didn't know who the chick was.

"Yo stop playing wit me!" The girl barked, "Why the fuck you ain't been returning my calls? I know you've been getting my messages."

"What messages?"

"Yo listen." The girl snorted, "I just got out the hospital from having *your* motherfucking baby, so the least you could do is return my calls!"

"You ain't just get out the hospital from having my baby." Live Wire said looking at the chick like she was insane. "Better go and try to pin that baby on another nigga."

The chick looked like she was getting ready to say some fly shit, when the old man stepped up, "Listen." The old man began, "I'm not gon sit here and let you disrespect my daughter. Now there's two ways we can resolve this, one you can be a father to *your* child, or two you can take this ass whipping I'm bout to put on you." The old man said taking an aggressive step forward.

Live Wire gave the old man a comical look. "You can't be serious."

"I'm bout to show you just how serious I am, you jive turkey." The old man lunged towards Live Wire. He tried to do some old take down move, but his attempt was denied when a powerful right hook connected with his chin knocking him out cold.

"Stupid ass old man!" Live Wire barked, cleared his throat and spit a glob of phlegm down onto the old man's face. Immediately the chick with the blond weave ran over to her father's aid.

Sparkle walked over and snuffed the chick in the side of her face, just cause. "Stay the fuck away from my man bitch." She spat before Live Wire pulled her away from the father daughter couple. "Come on we out." Live Wire said when they reached his brand new sleek Benz.

In a swift motion, Sparkle turned and swung on Live Wire throwing a flurry of wild punches. A few of the punches connected and landed, until Live Wire finally grabbed Sparkle's arms and spun her around forcefully pinning her back up against the Benz. "Fuck is you doing?" He asked confused on why he was being hit.

"Get your fucking hands off me!" Sparkle struggled to get free. "It's always something with you and these bitches and I'm sick of it!"

"I don't even know that chick." Live Wire lied with a straight face. He had so many women that it was beginning to get hard to keep track of all of them.

"Aight watch!" Sparkle nodded her head up and down. "I got you!"

"Aight watch what?"

"I'mma start treating you just how you treat me." Sparkle hissed. "You can dish it; now let's see if you can take it."

"What I told you about hoe talking?" Live Wire said as his hand shot out and gripped around Sparkle's throat. "You wanna go give that pussy away? Huh?"

"No Daddy." Sparkle whispered as tears began to fall from her eyes. "I just want you to do right?"

Live Wire pulled Sparkle in close for a hug, he peered over her shoulder and saw a few of The Real Spades fishing through the old man' that lay knocked out on the concrete's pockets, while another member snatched the chick with the blonde hair's purse and almost took her shoulder off in the process.

"Yo listen."Live Wire palmed Sparkle's huge ass that felt as soft as pillows, "You gon have to stop with all this jealous shit. Who Daddy am I?"

"My daddy," Was Sparkle reply.

"Huh!?"

"My daddy!" Sparkle said a little louder.

"Well start acting like it before..." The sound of screeching tires, followed by more than one machine gun being fired filled the air as Live Wire quickly tackled Sparkle down to the ground. Live Wire's brand new Benz was the only thing that stood in between the gun men, him and Sparkle.

Bullets rocked and riddled the Benz as glass rained down on top of Live Wire and Sparkle's head. Seconds later the gun fire ended and the sound of screeching tires were the only thing that could be heard along with a few car alarms wailing.

"You alright?" Live Wire asked as he quickly helped Sparkle up to her feet. He looked up and saw a few of The Real Spades laid out in a pool of blood, as well as the chick with the blonde weave.

"I'm good." Sparkle replied doing her best to keep up with Live Wire. Live Wire didn't want to be nowhere around when the police showed up. He didn't know if they would be coming to lock him up or kill him, either way he wasn't about to chance it.

Sparkle flagged down a cab on the next corner and her and Live Wire quickly slid in the back seat and kept their heads as low as possible. During the ride Live Wire felt his cell phone vibrate, he glanced down at the screen and saw that he had a text message from Tori.

Tori: *I told you I wasn't the one to be fucked with.*

Live Wire replied instantly.

Live Wire: *Bitch when I catch ya white ass, I'mma show you how to truly violate a bitch.*

Tori: *The one thing you don't do is play with a woman's heart; you played me for a fool. Now I'mma show you what this little white girl is all about.*

Live Wire: *Listen bitch! When I catch you, it ain't gon be pretty.*

Tori: *I knew you were a clown the day I met you and now I'm gonna have your head blown off for all the women you've used and played with their hearts......you're going to pay.*

Live Wire: *I'm not hard to find. Just make sure you back up all this tough talk when I run into you.*

Tori: *I'm going to kill you and that fake ass ghetto Barbie doll girlfriend of yours.*

Live Wire: *Take a number and get in line.*

Now that Live Wire knew who was responsible for all the shooting, it wasn't nothing left to talk about. When him and Tori crossed paths it would be on, on sight. Live wire didn't dare tell Sparkle that Tori was the one responsible for the shooting cause he knew he'd never hear the end of it. The last thing he wanted to do was argue with Sparkle some more about another woman, all that was on his mind was getting home so he could eat Sparkle's pussy, have a drink and go to sleep.

Chapter Twenty Two

Playing For Keeps

Victor Gambino sat at the bar enjoying a few drinks. It wasn't often that he went out, but tonight he said fuck it, he was tired of being cooped up in his motel room all night doing nothing. Victor wasn't a heavy drinker, but when he did drink nine times out of ten he always winded up twisted before the night was over.

As Victor sat enjoying his drink, he noticed a Jamaican man with filthy nappy looking dreads take the stool next to him. Something about the man didn't sit right with Victor, but he paid it no mind and continued to get his drink on.

"Damn Breadrin." The man with the filthy dreads huffed staring at Victor with a mean look on his face. "You just gon fart while I'm sitting right here and not say excuse me?"

"Fuck is you talking about?" Victor huffed. He didn't know the dread man from a hole in the wall and wasn't in the mood for a back and forth conversation. "I didn't fart; it's probably your dirty ass dreads that smelling like that." He capped.

"Don't disrespect me." Filthy dread barked, "Trust, you no wan go there with me."

"Okay dread." Victor tried to brush the drunk Jamaican off, before his temper got the best of him and he ended up going overboard and getting carried away. "Matter of fact, bartender let me get a drink for dread over here." He called out to the bartender.

Seconds later the bartender sat a drink in front of the Jamaican. The Jamaican eyes the drink for a second before lifting it up to his nose, taking a strong wift, without warning the Jamaican turned and tossed the drink in Victor's face, then snuffed him off the bar stool.

"Me not de one to play wit pussy boy!" The Jamaican barked back peddling towards the exit.

Victor wiped his eyes, removed his .45 from the holster on the small of his back and started blasting

Boc! Boc! Boc! Boc! Boc!

As soon as the Jamaican man reached the exit one of Victor's bullets exploded in his gut forcing him out the front door.

Loud screams erupted from inside the bar as Victor shook off the blow and headed outside to finish the foolish Jamaican man off. He planned on making the Jamaican wish that he was never born.

Victor stepped foot outside the bar and spotted the Jamaican hunched over down on one knee, he slid behind the Jamaican pressed his .45 to the back of his head and pulled the trigger.

Boc!

When Victor looked up he saw movement out in the parking lot, immediately he knew the man with the filthy dreads had been a decoy and he was being set up.

Bobby Dread appeared out of the darkness in the parking lot with a two handed grip on his A.K. 47 and several wild looking Jamaican niggaz with him.

Victor turned and took off in a sprint, firing several reckless shots over his shoulder as he made a dash for the entrance of the bar. Victor Gambino made it to the door of the bar before he was gunned down. A bullet hit him in the hip causing his body to jerk and spin around. A second bullet exploded in his shoulder spinning him in the opposite direction and the third bullet hit Victor in the back forcing him back into the bar.

Three bullets in his body still didn’t stop Victor. He crawled at a snail’s pace looking for an escape route. He refused to die in the streets like a hoodlum. Victor crawled until he couldn't crawl anymore and finally blacked out.

Chapter Twenty Three

A Time To Kill

Wolf had little Sunshine in his arms and gently rocked her while she slept peacefully in his arms. Sunshine's birth had Wolf feeling like he finally had a reason to live, a purpose in life, he had never loved anyone or anything as much as he loved his little princess.

"I swear you're going to spoil that little girl." Ivy looked on from the couch with a warm smile on her face. She loved how lovingly Wolf was when it came to Sunshine, she knew all along that he would be a good father, but to see him interact with Sunshine in person made her heart melt.

"I'm going to spoil this little girl until the day I die." Wolf said seriously. One of his loyal Spade members was keeping him updated on the destruction that The Big Show and The Spades were out there doing in the streets, but that was no longer his concern, his main and only concern was the little girl that laid curled in his arms.

"Why don't you put the baby in her crib so we can enjoy some of this quiet time while we got the chance." Ivy suggested. With the new baby and all Ivy and Wolf rarely had time to spend alone with one another. "I want to see that new Tyler Perry joint that I bought on DVD the other day. You wit it?"

"You already know." Wolf said as he disappeared inside Sunshine's room and laid her down in her crib. He placed a kiss on her cheek, then joined Ivy back out in the living room.

"I'm all yours." Wolf smiled.

"You love me?" Ivy asked out of nowhere, with a devilish grin on her face.

"Oh lord." Wolf shook his head, "What do you want?" He asked knowing that Ivy only asked that question when she wanted something.

"Just answer the question do you love me?" Ivy paused.

"I'll play along." Wolf laughed. "Yes baby I love you to death, now what do you want?"

"You love me enough to run to the store and get me some Popeye's before we start this movie?" Ivy placed her hands together in a praying position. "Pleeeeaaaase?"

"I got you baby." Wolf said as he slipped on some sweat pants, some house shoes, grabbed his keys and headed for the door.

"And hurry up." Ivy called out. "Five wings, fries, and a Hi-C. Thanks I love you."

"Not only are you bossing me around, but on top of that now you rushing me."

Wolf shook his head. "Why me Lord?" He said looking up at the ceiling before walking out the front door to go get Ivy some chicken.

"I love him to death." Ivy said to herself as she smiled for no reason. This was the happiest she had ever been in her entire life. Wolf treated her like a Queen and made sure she and little Sunshine didn't want or need for anything. Even if Wolf was dead broke, Ivy would still love Wolf, he was a good man with a good heart and nowadays that was a rare combination to find in a man. Wolf gave the word a *good* man some meaning.

The sound of someone messing around with the locks on the front door snapped Ivy out of her thoughts. She quickly ran to the door and snatched it open thinking that it was Wolf coming back because he had forgotten something. On the other side of the door stood a man in all black crouched down with a sharp object in his hand attempting to pick the lock.

Before Ivy got a chance to scream, a gloved hand shot out and covered her mouth. The big man wearing a suit then forced Ivy back into the house, picked her up and violently slammed her down to the floor with extreme force, then several other men wearing all black stormed in the house and duct taped Ivy's wrist and ankles.

"What the hell is going on?" Ivy yelled not able to recognize any of the men that filled her living room, but from their all black dress code they looked like members from The Spades, but why would The Spades be here and why would they be using such force with her? Ivy's questions were answered when she saw Pauleena step foot through the front door with The Big Show close on her heels.

"So." Pauleena began with a smile looking down at Ivy, "You're the special woman that got Wolf to turn his back on The Spades."

"What the fuck you want?" Ivy growled.

"I'm so sorry. How rude of me, let me introduce myself." Pauleena knelt down and punched Ivy dead in her face. "I'm Pauleena, now be a good girl and tell me where I can find Wolf and I'll *think* about letting you keep your life."

"Fuck you!" Ivy spat, then turned and looked up at The Big Show. "And you." She snarled, "you should be ashamed of yourself, Wolf treated you like a brother, gave you a job when you had nothing and this is what you do to him? You lead the devil straight to our front door?"

"This ain't personal sweetie." The Big Show said with a greasy look in his eyes."This is business and if you know what's best for you, then you'll tell us where that pussy Wolf is hiding."

"Wolf would never hide from someone like you." Ivy said in a defensive tone. Wolf was done with that lifestyle, so Ivy didn't understand why Pauleena and The Big Show wouldn't leave him alone and just let him be. It was like they were upset that he had made it out of the game with his life as well as his freedom.

Ivy lay on the floor while she heard The Spades search through the house like the Feds looking for Wolf or anything of value. She heard things breaking and the sound of furniture moving, when she saw a muscular man come from the back with little Sunshine in his arms, she almost died.

"No, no, no." Ivy said. "Please give me my baby. Take me, kill me, but don't hurt my baby." She begged.

"I didn't know that Wolf was a father." Pauleena said taking little Sunshine from the man's arms instantly little Sunshine began crying at the top of her lungs, it was as if the baby could feel that Pauleena was evil. "Aw don't cry." Pauleena said in a baby voice.

"I swear to god if you lay a finger on my baby...." A swift kick to Ivy's face silenced her.

"You better tell me where I can find Wolf right now or shit bout to get real ugly." Pauleena warned. The look in her eyes told Ivy that she wasn't fucking around.

"Please don't do this." Ivy begged. She knew if she was to give Wolf up that Pauleena more than likely would still kill all of them, that was just the type of person she was. "Pauleena I'm talking to you woman to woman, that's my daughter you're holding in your arms, please put her back in her crib, kill me, take me hostage or whatever it is you going to do, but please leave my daughter alone....please."

"Oh, you must think this shit is a game!" Pauleena spat as she let little Sunshine dangle from her hand, she held her with one hand by the baby's little shirt. "You gon learn today!" Pauleena headed over to the microwave and open it. "Bring that bitch over here!"

Several Spades grabbed Ivy and set her down in a chair, then bound her down to the chair with duct tape giving her a front row seat.

Pauleena roughly placed little Sunshine in the microwave and slammed the door shut. "You got five seconds to start talking....four." She said jumping the count.

"Please." Ivy cried, "Why are you doing this?" She could hear little Sunshine's muffled screaming coming from inside the microwave.

"Five!" Pauleena said then sat the timer on the microwave to 30:00 minutes. "Tell me where Wolf is right now or else I'm going to press start." Pauleena said placing her finger on the start button.

"Okay, okay!" Ivy screamed. "Wolf went to the store to get me some chicken. Please just let my baby go, please take her out that microwave." Ivy felt bad for giving up Wolf's whereabouts, but she was just trying to save her daughter's life by any means necessary. Little Sunshine's screams were getting louder and louder by the second. Hearing her daughter cry at the top of her lungs and it was nothing she could do about it that was driving Ivy crazy.

Pauleena gave Ivy a sad look, then shook her head. "I have your daughter in a fucking microwave and the best lie you could come up with was that Wolf is at the store buying you some chicken.........What I told you about playing with me?"

What!? No wait, I'm not lying!" Ivy tried to explain, but it was too late. Pauleena pressed the start button on the microwave and instantly the inside of the microwave lit up, as the plate that little Sunshine lay on began to spin slowly.

"Noooooooooooo!"Ivy screamed at the top of her lings as she struggled to break free from the duct tape that had her bound down to the chair, the sight of little Sunshine spinning around in the microwave was killing Ivy literally. Ivy looked over at The Big Show. "Stop her please!" She begged, "Please press the stop button Big Show pleeeeese!"

The Big Show had a sad look on his face as he broke eye contact with Ivy and looked down at the floor. He knew Pauleena was taking it too far, but he wasn't foolish enough to challenge Pauleena's decision. He had planned to come over kill, Wolf and leave. All this other shit wasn't his cup of tea. "Excuse me." he said and exited the house with his head hung low.

The sound of little Sunshine's skin sizzling attacked Ivy's ears, as the smell of burning flesh filled the air.

"I swear to god on my life bitch I'm going to kill you!" Ivy growled looking Pauleena in the eyes.

"Bitch!" Pauleena exploded as she ran over and unleashed a combination of hard punches to Ivy's exposed face, until finally Big Ock pulled her up off Ivy.

"Come on it's time to go!" Big Ock said escorting Pauleena out the door.

"Bitch fuck you and that pussy Wolf, I ain't hard to find." Pauleena huffed before she was escorted out the front door, leaving Ivy all alone in the house.

Ivy cried and wept silently as she could no longer hear little Sunshine's cry. Her little soldier had fought as hard as she could, but there was only so much her little body could take.

Ivy sat with her head hung low as the microwave beeped continuously announcing that whatever was cooking in the microwave was *done*. Ivy said a silent prayer as she heard the front door open.

"Sorry baby the lines were mad long, they ran out of wings so I had to wait for the next batch to get done." Wolf walked in carrying a bag of chicken. "I started to go to KFC, but...." Wolf's words got caught in his throat when he saw Ivy sitting near the kitchen taped down to a chair. He dropped the bag of chicken and ran over to Ivy's side.

"Baby what happened? You alright? What happened?" Wolf asked, but Ivy wouldn't respond. "Why the fuck you not talking!? What happened?"

Instead of replying Ivy broke out into even more tears. Immediately Wolf's mind went to little Sunshine, he quickly ran to her bedroom where he had left her. He stormed back to the living room with a hurt and scared look on his face.

"Where is sunshine?" Wolf asked. "And what the fuck is that smell?"

Again Ivy didn't reply she just cried.

"Talk motherfucker!" Wolf yelled in Ivy's face as he began to shake her. "Where is Sunshine?"

Ivy nodded towards the microwave. Wolf's eyes followed the direction that Ivy had nodded in. "No, no, no." Wolf said in a soft voice as he slowly walked over to the microwave and slowly opened the door. The site of what was left of little Sunshine caused Wolf to throw up. "Urggggh." He heaved over and over again.

Wolf walked over to the knife rack and removed a sharp steak knife; he then walked over and cut the tape from Ivy's wrist and ankles. Wolf squatted down and looked in Ivy's eyes, "Who did this?" he asked through clenched teeth.

"Pauleena." Ivy said, then got up and disappeared in their bedroom.

Wolf walked over to the couch, sat down and buried his face in his hands, he had only went to get some chicken for Ivy, he never in a million years would of thought that while he was at the store his daughter would be losing her life because of his past. Wolf cried like a baby, as his mind began to wonder, how did Pauleena find out where he lived?

The sound of Ivy coming out the bedroom snapped Wolf out of his thoughts. He looked up and saw Ivy standing there holding a 9mm in her hand. For a second Wolf thought that Ivy was about to shoot him, because it was his past that had gotten their daughter killed, but to his surprise she held the gun out towards him. Wolf reluctantly accepted the gun.

"You been dying to go back to New York, well now here's your chance." Ivy whispered. "You just promise me two things."

"Anything," Was Wolf's response.

"Promise me you're going to kill that bitch Pauleena."

"And what else?" Wolf asked curiously.

"Promise me that you'll let me help you." Ivy said with a serious look on her face.

"No." Wolf said quickly. "I've already hurt you and my family enough."

"I've never been defiant to you ever Wolf, but I'm afraid that this is the one time I'm going to have to go against you." Ivy told him. "I'm not letting you go out and fight an army all by yourself." She snapped, and picked up the lamp and tossed it across the room. "Your fucking past has come back to haunt us, and I don't give a fuck what you say, I'm going to kill that bitch Pauleena" Ivy yelled hysterically. "And I'm going to do this with or without you" Ivy went to rip the 70 inch flat screen down off the wall, but Wolf quickly stopped her, by pulling her in close for a much needed hug.

"Our little Sunshine was innocent, she ain't cause no harm to no one, why?...why" Ivy cried. "My baby"

"Its going to be okay" Wolf said as tears ran freely down his face. "I promise I'm going to fix this" He promised.

"I'm coming with you" Ivy told him. "It's one thing you don't fuck with, and that's a mother's baby, that's word on my life I'm going to kill that bitch Pauleena, are you with me or what?"

"I'm about to paint the whole motherfucking city red!" Wolf growled. "Them motherfuckers want the Wolf, then that's what I'm going to give them!" He said staring at the gun in his hand with a crazed look in his eyes. Pauleena and anyone affiliated with her had a big problem on their hands, they now had a blood thirsty Wolf on their trail.

Wolf looked up at Ivy with a sick grin on his face. "This shit about to get real bloody and messy, you bout to see the type of shit that you might not be prepared for....you riding or what?"

Ivy matched Wolf's stare and answered."Until the motherfucking wheels fall off!"

To be continued

Tears of a Hustler 6
"The Return of The Wolf" Coming Soon!

Contact info: silkwhite212@yahoo.com

Now Available:
Paperback & E-Book

On Our Bookshelf

THE TEFLON QUEEN
A NOVEL BY
SILK WHITE

GOOD 2 GO PUBLISHING PRESENTS
NEVER BE THE SAME
A NOVEL BY
SILK WHITE

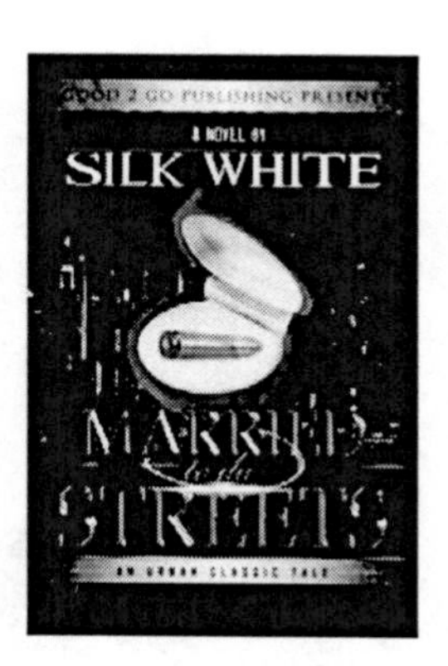
GOOD 2 GO PUBLISHING PRESENTS
A NOVEL BY
SILK WHITE
MARRIED to the STREETS
AN URBAN CLASSIC TALE

TEARS OF A HUSTLER
A NOVEL BY
SILK WHITE

TEARS OF A HUSTLER 2
A NOVEL BY
SILK WHITE

GOOD 2 GO PUBLISHING PRESENTS
TEARS OF A HUSTLER 3
A NOVEL BY
SILK WHITE

Good2Go Films Presents

To order films please go to www.good2gofilms.com
To order books, please fill out the order form below:

Name:

____

Address:

____

____

City: ____________________ State: ______ Zip Code: ____________________

Phone:

____

Email:

____

Method Payment: Check ☐ VISA ☐ MASTERCARD ☐

Credit Card#:

____

Name as it appears on card:

____

Signature:

____

Item Name	Price	Qty	Amount
He Loves Me, He Loves You Not - Mychea	$13.95		
He Loves Me, He Loves You Not 2 - Mychea	$13.95		
Married To Da Streets – Silk White	$13.95		
Never Be The Same – Silk White	$13.95		
Tears of a Hustler - Silk White	$13.95		
Tears of a Hustler 2 - Silk White	$13.95		
Tears of a Hustler 3 - Silk White	$13.95		
Tears of a Hustler 4- Silk White	$13.95		
The Teflon Queen – Silk White	$13.95		
The Teflon Queen 2 – Silk White	$13.95		
Young Goonz – Reality Way	$13.95		

Subtotal:			
Tax:			
Shipping (Free) U.S. Media Mail:			
Total:			

Make Checks Payable To:
Good2Go Publishing
7311 W Glass Lane
Laveen, AZ 85339